# Every Duke Has His Price

### Dukes in Danger
### Book 5

## Emily E K Murdoch

## ARE YOU SIGNED UP FOR DRAGONBLADE'S BLOG?

You'll get the latest news and information on exclusive giveaways, exclusive excerpts, coming releases, sales, free books, cover reveals and more.

Check out our complete list of authors, too!

No spam, no junk. That's a promise!

### Sign Up Here

www.dragonbladepublishing.com

*Dearest Reader;*

*Thank you for your support of a small press. At Dragonblade Publishing, we strive to bring you the highest quality Historical Romance from some of the best authors in the business. Without your support, there is no 'us', so we sincerely hope you adore these stories and find some new favorite authors along the way.*

*Happy Reading!*

*CEO, Dragonblade Publishing*

# Additional Dragonblade books by Author Emily E K Murdoch

### Dukes in Danger Series
Don't Judge a Duke by His Cover (Book 1)
Strike While the Duke is Hot (Book 2)
The Duke is Mightier than the Sword (Book 3)
A Duke in Time Saves Nine (Book 4)
Every Duke Has His Price (Book 5)

### Twelve Days of Christmas
Twelve Drummers Drumming
Eleven Pipers Piping
Ten Lords a Leaping
Nine Ladies Dancing
Eight Maids a Milking
Seven Swans a Swimming
Six Geese a Laying
Five Gold Rings
Four Calling Birds
Three French Hens
Two Turtle Doves
A Partridge in a Pear Tree

### The De Petras Saga
The Misplaced Husband (Book 1)
The Impoverished Dowry (Book 2)
The Contrary Debutante (Book 3)
The Determined Mistress (Book 4)
The Convenient Engagement (Book 5)

### The Governess Bureau Series
A Governess of Great Talents (Book 1)
A Governess of Discretion (Book 2)

A Governess of Many Languages (Book 3)
A Governess of Prodigious Skill (Book 4)
A Governess of Unusual Experience (Book 5)
A Governess of Wise Years (Book 6)
A Governess of No Fear (Novella)

**Never The Bride Series**
Always the Bridesmaid (Book 1)
Always the Chaperone (Book 2)
Always the Courtesan (Book 3)
Always the Best Friend (Book 4)
Always the Wallflower (Book 5)
Always the Bluestocking (Book 6)
Always the Rival (Book 7)
Always the Matchmaker (Book 8)
Always the Widow (Book 9)
Always the Rebel (Book 10)
Always the Mistress (Book 11)
Always the Second Choice (Book 12)
Always the Mistletoe (Novella)
Always the Reverend (Novella)

**The Lyon's Den Series**
Always the Lyon Tamer

**Pirates of Britannia Series**
Always the High Seas

**De Wolfe Pack: The Series**
Whirlwind with a Wolfe

# CHAPTER ONE

*September 30, 1810*

T HE ROAR OF the pub exploding with joy that he had lost, and badly, was hardly music to Hugh Shardlow, Duke of Martock's ears.

"Damn and—"

But he managed to hold his tongue. With difficulty.

It was fortunate perhaps that he had spoken under his breath. It was even more fortunate—or unfortunate, depending on one's perspective—that he had started to swear in English, a language rarely spoken here.

He had spent the last two weeks wandering, thinking he would perhaps run into an Englishman in these godforsaken French inns, all without success. But his failure until now had at least benefited him. It would never do for his opponent to realize what he'd been about to say.

His opponent, a man who had been introduced with the single name Pierre, was glaring. Hugh grinned as though he did not care he had lost his second to last coin in the world.

"Good hand," Hugh said in flawless French.

Pierre grunted. Through the dirty dark curls hanging low across his forehead, greed glinted in his eyes. "Another?"

Hugh hesitated.

He was not normally one to turn down an opportunity for another hand of cards. In the best halls of London, even some of the less prestigious ones, he was known for his splendid ability to guess precisely what another man would bid, and if he was bluffing. The skill had him banned from the Dulverton Club, though Hugh had protested he'd not been cheating.

He was just good at reading people. Should he truly be punished for such an art?

But he was, and so he had taken his clever hands and skill with a deck elsewhere, and made plenty of money. But it hadn't been enough.

"Well?" snapped Pierre. "Another hand?"

Hugh was suddenly very conscious their seemingly small and inconsequential game in a corner of a dark inn in the middle of nowhere France seemed to be attracting a great deal more attention than expected.

There was a man at the bar casting them covert looks. Two men who'd been having a conversation at the next table over paused to listen to his response. And that man by the door, with the very visible pistol...

Hugh sighed. It was the oldest trick in the book. He should have been expecting it.

Well, they were determined to rid him of absolutely all coin, that was clear—he may as well allow them to do so through a game of cards. It would at least prevent him from having to fight them. His bare-knuckle boxing days were rather rusty.

"Of course, another hand," Hugh said with a smile he did not feel.

Pierre's—if that was his real name—smile was far more genuine. "Excellent! What do you bet?"

With great frustration—the whole purpose to come here was to attempt to win more coin, not lose it!—Hugh dug in his waistcoat pocket, his coat buttons undone but the coat itself still around his shoulders. He poured the contents of his pockets onto the table. Pierre peered down.

An English shilling. A button, not one from anything he was wearing. A small tinderbox with a coat of arms.

Hugh quickly turned the tinderbox over, but Pierre's eyes were sharper than that.

"Oh, a stolen little trinket, I see!" he said with glee. "Well, you can barter with—"

"That's tin, not stolen, and mine," Hugh said quietly, a dark sort of anger he could not quite hide. "Thank you."

Without breaking his gaze from the card shark, he picked up the tinderbox and placed it back in his pocket.

Which did not explain why his heart was beating so fast, Hugh tried not to think. Well, he'd been a fool to bring that out. What if—no, no one in this French backwater would have recognized that crest. Quite a few Englishmen would not recognize it, even gentlemen. *Still.* It was madness to give anyone the chance.

Hugh Shardlow may have spent the last six months in France, but the Duke of Martock…that was another story. That particular part of his identity he had kept quite hidden.

The ransom for his safe return alone would cost a fair few more shillings than he had on him, and the shame it would bring the family…

"Well, a shilling isn't much," Pierre said grumpily.

And Hugh saw his chance. He should have known the minute he walked into this inn that it would not suffice. His desires were far more expensive than what he could have won here—assuming the other man hadn't cheated.

He would simply have to make his way elsewhere, that was all.

"In that case, I will bid you a good—"

"Did I say you could leave?" Pierre spat, voice threatening and brows furrowed.

The two men at the table beside them half rose to their feet, one of them revealing—

Hugh groaned. *A knife. Of course.*

"I did not say I would not play. You were the one who suggested my stakes were insufficient," he pointed out.

But to no avail. Obviously, they had decided his paltry shilling was more than enough to play for. Perhaps even to fight for. If he was foolish enough, to die for.

Hugh groaned inwardly, but there was nothing for it. He had brought this on himself by not putting aside enough funds to pay for what he so desperately wished—and despite his prowess with the cards, an honest man could never beat a cheat.

Not that he was idiot enough to accuse any man of cheating in a place like this…

"I say we play," Pierre said darkly.

Hugh sighed. He could fight his way out. He had a knife similar to the one being carefully not concealed by Pierre's friend. He was probably better than the man at wielding it.

But that wasn't the problem. The problem was that there were five of them, at least, and only one of him. Not great odds. So, he would lose the shilling. But he would keep his life.

"Play then," he said nonchalantly, as though he hardly cared either way.

Pierre grinned. "Excellent."

It was over swiftly. Hugh knew it would be and he put up very little fuss, not bothering to bid on the right cards, unconcerned when his hand did not improve. What difference would it make? He was going to lose the shilling anyway.

Pierre grinned. "I have won!"

Hugh shrugged. "Good for you, man. Have a pleasant evening."

He thought, just for a moment, he may not be permitted to leave. Any idiot with half an eye could have spotted the real silver of the tinderbox. Perhaps they would rob him for it. Perhaps they would beat him just for the indignation of having attempted to refuse the game.

But though Hugh was ready for them, ensuring he was balanced perfectly on the balls of his feet as he rose, there appeared to be no need. Pierre's gaze was already raking across the gloomy inn for another victim.

And so Hugh was permitted to approach the bar and take a long, deep breath.

Not that it mattered. Though his mouth watered, the scent of ale rising in the air, he could not pay for it. A drink would have to be enjoyed another—

"On the house," grunted the innkeeper, pushing forward a tankard brimming with ale.

Hugh curled his fingers around the handle and drank eagerly. It was the first thing he had drunk all day. Or was it already tomorrow? His pocket watch had been pawned a long time ago. It was impossible to tell in this dank gloom.

"Thirsty," grunted the innkeeper in French.

Hugh nodded. He probably shouldn't drink too fast; he'd not eaten either. The last thing he needed was to leave his wits behind at the bar as he attempted to leave.

"What are you doing here, English?" the innkeeper asked suddenly.

A twist of frustration and just a hint of boredom soared through Hugh's chest. It was the same old question, one that probably he should have expected.

After all, there was a war on.

"I'm stuck here," Hugh said honestly, finding over the weeks that the truth was the swiftest way to end the conversation. "I came here with plenty of money, now I have none."

He took a slow sip of his ale. And why did that sting so badly? Was it because he was a duke, accustomed to always having his way?

He had never been one to carry money. *Actual coins?* Hugh would have laughed at the thought six months ago. Why, he had people for that! Bills came to the house, and bills were paid. His butler, his steward, they both managed his estates, his staff, his expenses.

Before he had taken the ship across the Channel, Hugh could not recall the last time he had seen an actual coin. Now here he was, without any, and in desperate need.

*Well, not desperate need,* he tried to tell himself as he looked out across the inn. It was just…well. Life would be a lot easier with coin. He was unlikely to gain any from the people here either. Hugh had even considered begging—an absolute disgrace, particularly if word ever reached English shores that the Duke of Martock…

Unthinkable.

"I was a fool to come here anyway," he said aloud, surprising himself as well as the innkeeper. "But I was bored."

"Bored?" repeated the innkeeper.

Hugh laughed bitterly. "Yes, it does sound foolish when you say it like that. But yes, I was bored. I had tired of life, at least I thought I had, and I was determined to do something, go somewhere that would be more exciting."

Oh, what an imbecile he had been.

Still, everything was clear in hindsight, wasn't it? Though even now, Hugh struggled to remember the precise thoughts which had led him to embark on a boat toward a war torn country where he had no friends, no plans, and no idea what to do with himself.

And the damned lack of plan had led him to…here.

"What was it about England that bored you so much?" asked the innkeeper, serving one of Pierre's friends—a man who glared curiously. "Your business, it was not going well?"

Hugh gave a dry laugh. "Something like that."

Well, being a duke was dull, wasn't it? And it was almost like a business. Money came in, money came out, and you had to make sure more stayed in your coffers than left the building. You had employees, of a sort. You even had to find someone to hand it down to.

Hugh snorted. His father would have been horrified that he was six and twenty and unmarried. No heirs? No one to pass down the dishonorable name of Martock?

And that was precisely why he had avoided it.

"No wife?" the innkeeper asked, as though he could read the duke's mind. "Children?"

"Nothing of the sort," said Hugh, trying not to rush through his drink. It may be the last thing he consumed for some time. "In fact, if I were in London right now, I…"

His voice trailed away. What would he be doing?

*Dancing to dull music with an even duller partner at Almack's, probably,* he thought ruefully. Forced to listen to old biddies chant the exquisite taste of their daughters as though they were being sold at market. Nod along to the very boring political discussions raging.

Anything, in fact, rather than actually enjoy himself.

"Ah," said the innkeeper, nodding in a knowing way that Hugh was not sure he liked. "So you have escaped a marriage."

Hugh snorted. "Something like that. But, of course, I don't have much to offer, and so there weren't many vying for my attention."

That was a lie.

But it was a lie he rather liked. It was pleasant to think he could one day return to London, to England at all, and avoid the sort of desperate marriage mart nonsense every other gentleman had to endure.

After all, what did he have to offer? Money, he supposed. A title.

But the wrong sort of title. No respectable woman, once they discovered he was a Martock, was entranced.

Hugh recalled his last conversation in society before he had left England.

"Well, Your Grace, I hope you will accept my papa's invitation to dine," said a rather sprightly Miss Lymington.

And for a moment, Hugh had been tempted. Her beauty had not been exaggerated, and it was easy to see her company would be most pleasant. And then—

"My dear, come away now." A woman who must have been Miss Lymington's mother had bustled up, a crease in her brow and her eyes darting.

That told him enough.

"But I am conversing with His Grace," Miss Lymington had started.

But her hands had been immediately captured by her mother. "I said, come away! That's not just any duke—that's the Duke of Martock!"

And Hugh could remember, even months later, the look of shock and surprise on the young lady's face. The horror that she had inadvertently been speaking to one of the most dastardly and ill-thought of men in the *ton*. And the curiosity, yes, the desperate desire to know why.

"Running away, eh?"

"I am not running away," Hugh said sharply, bestowing a glare upon the innkeeper.

The man swallowed. "No offense meant, of course."

"Hmph."

Though his blood was starting to boil, Hugh managed to calm himself. Looking away from the innkeeper helped. Looking into the tankard of ale helped even more.

Because the man was right, in a way. Oh, he would never admit to such. Dukes did not run away, and he certainly would not. Except that he had, hadn't he?

He certainly wasn't running toward anything—there was nothing in France that Hugh wanted. And he did wish to return home, though precisely how he would manage to do such a thing without a single penny to rub between his fingers, he did not know.

"You don't have any friends?"

Hugh chuckled with a wry shake of his head. "Few that would own me now."

There were probably a few members of the Dulverton Club who would raise a subscription to have him returned home,

Hugh thought grimly. But he was not sure if that could be called friendship. Half would do so to laugh in his face for getting himself into such a pickle. The other half would want their money back.

And that was the trouble with hiding his true identity. Dukes deserved, and usually got, respect. Men tramping across the French countryside rarely gained anything save pity. And even that was thin on the ground at the moment.

This was a country at war, Hugh tried to remind himself. There was more going on than just his pathetic attempt to have an adventure, which had completely gone awry.

"You know, I am surprised you have not gone back to England," said the innkeeper lazily, wiping a tankard with a moldy-looking rag. "With the war going so badly."

Hugh smiled despite himself. No matter what was happening in the war—and information was vague to say the least, and most untrustworthy—the French always said they were winning.

Even if they weren't.

"Don't you want to go back?"

Hugh hesitated. This innkeeper was far too inquisitive for his own good—or perhaps he had just spent too long on the road, and had forgotten what it was to have someone genuinely interested in him.

Spending the last six months alone in brothels, gambling hells, and avoiding battles was eventually going to tire, yes. But he was too ashamed to admit he had no friends, no money, and no way of getting himself across the Channel.

No man would wish to admit that, let alone a duke.

"I'll go back when I want to," he said aloud, his voice harsher than expected.

The innkeeper shrugged. "Whatever you say."

And as though Hugh's conversation had bored him, he drifted away along the bar and struck up a conversation in his thick French guttural accent with another man.

Hugh let out a long, slow breath he had not quite noticed he had been holding. Well, he had managed it. A conversation with someone during which he had not, mostly, embarrassed himself. He hadn't lost any money, or made any promises he had no intention of keeping. And he had not revealed his true identity.

That wasn't bad going, really.

The trouble was, Hugh mused as he drained the last dregs of the ale and wished he hadn't, he didn't have any idea what to do next. He hadn't heard an English voice in days, and now he had no money at all. It was going to be almost impossible to earn enough on the card tables to secure a passage back to England.

And that left him here. In a foreign land, with no food, no friends, and—

"Absolutely outrageous!" came a voice, light and airy. "No, really, you simply must let go. I have very little to—"

Hugh was tired. And he had drunk a very large tankard of ale in a very short period of time, and on an empty stomach too. Which was probably why it took him a little over a minute to realize three things.

Firstly, the voice he had heard was a woman. *A woman, in here?*

Secondly, the voice had not been speaking in French. She had been speaking English.

And thirdly, he desperately needed to turn around and see what sort of English woman had managed to find herself at an inn like this.

Slowly, Hugh placed the empty tankard onto the bar and turned on his heels.

His mouth fell open.

There, standing in the doorway and attempting most genteel-ly to disentangle her hand with that of a beggarwoman, was the most beautiful woman he had ever seen.

# CHAPTER TWO

"**A**BSOLUTELY OUTRAGEOUS! NO, really, you simply must let go. I have very little to offer you!"

Beth tried to smile, but this was more than she could possibly take. Could this day not just end? Why did it have to continue on and on, each hour bringing something more disastrous than the next?

"Please m'lady," said the old woman, her dirty fingernails clenched tight onto Beth's hand. "I just want—"

It was fortunate indeed that her French was far superior to most, Beth thought as she fired back rapidly, "Take your hands off me, woman, or I promise you indeed there will be hell to pay!"

Not, perhaps, the most elegant thing she could have said, even Beth would admit. Not that she had anyone to admit it to.

Not for the first time, she wondered if this whole endeavor may have been easier if she had actually listened to Nancy for more than five minutes together. It certainly would have been easier if there were two of them. Or if she had accepted the suggestion of a servant. Or, in truth, had listened to her sister and not come at all.

The old woman let go of Beth and crept away.

Beth swallowed hard, trying to forget the encounter had ever happened. The point was, she had come here, and she was determined not to leave France until her plan was completed. She owed him that.

But before she had a moment to look around the inn and see whether her journey all this way had finally been worth it, a man stepped before her.

"Not lost, are you, my dear?" he said in French, a smile revealing three missing teeth.

Beth tried to smile, but it was a challenge.

She was absolutely exhausted. How long had she been on her feet—two days? Three? They were all starting to merge, her lack of sleep and lack of food starting to wear on her.

Going hungry was not an entirely unknown experience. There had been times, just after her father had died, that Beth had gone hungry to ensure Matthew had enough. Her brother had always seemed hungrier. She could carry on with very little, really, in the way of food.

That had been then.

Now, two days after a proper meal, Beth could feel the telltale signs of lightheadedness creeping into the edges of her mind.

But she had to stay focused—to find him. She must ensure she was not taken advantage of by Frenchmen, she thought fiercely as she looked at the man before her.

Not in *that* way, of course. This may be France, but still!

"You look lost to me, my pretty," said the man, taking a step closer. "And I think I can help you there."

Beth instinctively took a step backward. "I doubt it."

The trouble was, as her mind whirled, attempting to find a way out of her predicament, this was the same old story. Almost every day since she had stepped onto French soil, there had been a blaggard who thought her pretty and in need of rescue. And she wasn't.

In need of rescue, that was. Beth was not shy about her appearance. No matter what her sister said, she saw no harm in accepting that her dark raven curls and delicate figure were precisely what society said she should be.

It was her tongue, and her inability to keep it quiet, that was her trouble.

"You're all alone here, aren't you?" said the man, his eyes glinting.

Beth swallowed, and saw instantly that was a mistake. Admitting she was alone, unprotected, was not clever in the depths of France with winter approaching.

Her gaze darted about the inn, just in case there was a French gentleman here breaking a journey. *Perhaps he could help,* Beth could not help but think.

Unfortunately, it appeared she was to be disappointed. There were plenty of men here—at least, now that she came to think about it, there were only men here. And a few ladies in a state of undress…

Beth's heart sank. So, it was that sort of inn.

She had never come across one in England, but she was a lady in England, and there were certain places a lady would never go. Here in France, she'd had no choice.

The men here were certainly not gentlemen. Many of them were gambling, and Beth saw the glint of candlelight on knives in belts. She had thought of bringing a pistol, stealing one from her brother-in-law's study, but what was the point? She had no idea how to use it, and even in the thick of action, was not entirely sure whether she would.

To shoot at someone, to take a life…

A few leers were being cast her way now, and Beth tried to hold herself as rigid and unperturbed on the outside as possible. The last thing she wanted was for them to see just how tired she was. Just how alone. Just how frightened.

Her gaze fell on a man standing by the bar, perhaps the most suspicious of the lot. He was staring as though he had never seen a woman before.

Beth's gaze dropped to the floor. *No gentleman would look at a woman like that.*

If only Matthew was here. Her brother would know what to do—*but then*, Beth reminded herself, *if Matthew was here, my journey would be at an end.* Her task would be over, and all she would have to worry about was getting them both home safely.

"You've come a long way, haven't you, miss?"

Beth blinked. She had half-forgotten the unpleasant man standing before her. He was examining her with a look of delight, and not one she wished to ever see again.

She took another step back. "I think—"

"I think you should come with me and have a drink, pretty," interrupted the man with a gleam in his eye. "Don't you?"

Beth tried not to bite her lip. It was a childish habit, that was what Nancy always said, and worst of all, it would betray just how nervous she was. And she had walked into worse places like this, she tried to tell herself. And left to tell the tale.

*But not this tired*, a dark, small voice muttered at the back of her mind. Not with so many knives so obviously showing. And not with such a strange man like the one at the bar, staring as though he had seen a ghost. Why was he looking at her like that?

"I am looking for a man," Beth said desperately.

It was the wrong thing to say. The man leered. "I bet you are!"

"Not like that—a specific man, my brother," she said hastily, wishing to goodness she had thought for more than a split second about what she had said. "His name is—"

"I am sure we can find you someone of any name." The man tried to grab her hand.

Beth jerked her hand away, heart starting to patter painfully in her chest.

This had been a mistake. She should have waited until morning, until daylight. Everything looked better in the daylight, didn't it?

The trouble was, as she well knew, most of these men would be back home, on their farms, in their shops. This was the best time to ask as many people as possible if they had caught sight of a dazed, confused, injured, and lost English soldier.

Matthew Mead. Her brother.

"You'll enjoy y'self, I promise—"

"No," said Beth, and her voice caught in her throat as real panic entered her heart. The man had tried to grab her again, and this time, his fingers almost caught around her wrist. If she didn't do something soon—

"Ah, there you are," said a man in smooth, melodious French. "I've been looking for you everywhere."

Beth looked up, eyes wide. The grasping hands of the horrible man had gone, and in his place stood…

The man from the bar.

Beth swallowed. From a distance, she had not quite realized how tall he was. Or how broad. Had he been slouching? Was the place just so dimly lit it was impossible to tell?

She could tell now. Her entire vision appeared to be filled with the man who was still staring as though he had never seen a woman before, but it was…different. *Hungry.*

Her cheeks flushed. "Here I am?"

"You are English, aren't you?" he said, more quietly this time.

Beth refused to meet his eye. This was the last thing she needed—an Englishman looking for a bit of English companionship. Oh, she understood the desire to speak English. She was tired of French, tired of constantly having to reach for words, stumbling over verbs.

But that did not mean she was going to permit herself to look weak before him. Not only was it completely against her very nature, but if she was to ask the inhabitants of this inn if they had seen her brother, she needed to ensure she did not look vulnerable.

Now that would be dangerous.

"I am English, yes, sir," she said coldly. "Good day."

She almost managed to step completely around him, but he was quicker than she'd expected.

"Good day?"

"Yes, it is a polite way of saying I no longer wish to talk to you," Beth snapped.

Her temper would be the death of her. That was what her sister Nancy had always said, and she had never believed it until this moment.

Fire sparked in the man's eyes, fire Beth knew would not easily be dampened.

"Dear God, woman, you are a danger to yourself and others," he breathed, not taking his eyes from her. "Come on."

And before Beth could do anything, before she could cry out, argue, exclaim, or tell him precisely what he could do with his bad manners—

His hand was on her arm. His fingers curled around her wrist and he was pulling her. Beth was not strong enough to stop him, unable to fight against him, her mind so tired she could barely think as it was—

They were standing outside the inn.

Beth wrenched her wrist from his grip. "How dare you!"

"How dare I? How dare you!" said the man with a laugh.

They had fallen into English now. *So much easier to shout in,* Beth could not help but think. It was colder here, a light breeze chilling the hot rage threatening to overspill.

Perhaps it still would. The nerve of the man, laying a hand on her and pulling her away from where she needed to go! Did he not see she had no wish to converse with him? Had she not made it expressly clear—

"You could thank me, you know."

Beth's eyes widened. "Thank you?"

What on earth did the man, whoever he was, think he was doing? There was a smug sort of satisfaction on his face that Beth instantly loathed. One of those men who assumed whatever they did was right, that they could never be criticized for anything. A man, in fact.

Well, she'd had enough of that sort of treatment in London, Beth thought bitterly. She wasn't going to permit anyone to treat her like that here. France, England, it was all the same.

*Men!*

"And what if," Beth said icily, "there was someone in there who could help me? Did you think of that, for even one second?"

The man's laugh was grating. "What, you think someone in there could—woman, you're in France! Don't you know there's a war on?"

Beth swallowed hard as the pain of Matthew's disappearance rose in her chest. The pain was almost as bad as the first time she and Nancy had realized it. No letters, no news for weeks, and then that note from his captain. Injured. Missing. Presumed dead.

Well, no Mead woman was going to permit their brother to gad about France being injured. Not a chance in hell. Beth rather wished she could say the sentence aloud, but her breeding forbade it.

Perhaps once.

"There is not a chance in *hell*," Beth said, relishing the word, "that I will thank you, or leave here without speaking to—"

"You cannot be serious!"

He grabbed hold of her as she tried to walk past him back to the inn.

Beth shook him off, truly angry now. That was what the heat flaring in her stomach was, wasn't it? "What is your name, sir?"

The man hesitated, so Beth knew for a fact that when he spoke, the name would be a lie. Well, she should not have expected much better.

"Hugh," he said eventually. "Hugh Shardlow."

Beth forced a grimace of a smile. "There, you are introduced; you may go on your way now."

For a second time, she attempted to walk past him and toward the inn, and for a second time, she was rebuffed—this time by Mr. Shardlow stepping into her path.

"You should be grateful," he said in an irritatingly calm tone.

Beth tried to take a deep breath before she replied, but it was impossible. "Grateful? Grateful to you? I cannot comprehend what you think I should be grateful for!"

"Oh, I don't know, preventing you from being attacked by that man," said Mr. Shardlow easily. "I don't know your name, by the way."

Beth shot a glare up at his smug, irritating face. "And it will stay that way. For goodness sake, I have to go in there and—"

"Do you have a death wish?" interrupted the idiot. He pointed at the inn. "You would have to be mad to go back in there! You, a woman, an English woman—alone?"

It was all true, but that did not mean Beth had to like it. In fact, she rather disliked it, almost as much as she disliked him. It was most infuriating, the fact that she could not go anywhere she wished without comment or speculation. Indeed, if she had entered a similar inn in England, the *ton* would have the gossip before the next Almack's.

Something Nancy would not thank her for.

She was tired—and not just in body. Tired of people telling her what she could do and couldn't do. Tired of society's rules keeping her in a place she did not want to be. Tired of embroidery, and playing the piano, and not being allowed to do anything interesting at all.

No, she'd had enough of that with her sister. Even Nancy's marriage hadn't improved things. Oh, Byron wasn't too bad, she supposed. He had saved her life, which put him slightly in her favor.

*But still—the rules!*

Mr. Shardlow evidently believed he had somehow convinced her with the power of his wit, for a lazy smile slid across his face. "There, I knew you would see reason eventually. All women do when a man is able to explain things to them."

And the fire Beth had always hidden and never permitted to show, the anger she had been forced to carry for so long, the fear for her brother, the rage that she had been forbidden to do anything to help him, the exhaustion she felt in her very bones...

All combined and rose, sparking hot in her chest.

What she was about to do was probably a bad idea. No. Beth knew it was a terrible idea.

But as she stood here in the cold French night, knowing that somewhere out there was her brother, injured and alone, Beth knew there was little she wouldn't do to find him. Not after searching for so long.

She met Mr. Shardlow's eyes and stepped closer to him. Just a step, that was all that was needed; he was already so close. Beth was quite tall for a lady, but even she had to lean up on her tiptoes to attempt to look him in the eye.

"Mr. Shardlow," Beth said sweetly.

The man smiled, utterly ignorant of what she was about to say. "I still don't know your—"

"If you want to try to stop me, and I think you probably still do, well, that would be a mistake," Beth said, continuing in her sweetest tone as she smiled into the astonished man's eyes. "Because I am going back to that inn, and I will be continuing with my inquiries. And your pigheaded attempt to impress me has not worked, and—"

"Hang on, there!"

"And I have no wish to give you my name, listen to your advice, or heed you in any way," Beth continued, adoring the sense of power rushing through her as she gazed deeply into the man's blue eyes. Handsome eyes. No, she mustn't get distracted. "If you want to stop me, you'll have to lay a hand on me as I scream bloody murder, and you know? I don't think you've got the nerve. Have you?"

She held his gaze. It was not something she had expected to be in her power, but now she was so close, she realized it was easy. Just look a man in the eye boldly. Why had she never done it before?

Perhaps because it made a strange heat flow through her. Perhaps because her breathing was ragged, her shoulders shaking with the tension roaring through her.

Perhaps, and Beth was not entirely sure whether she had

dreamed it, but perhaps because she might have seen a flicker of desire there in Mr. Shardlow's eyes. It was there one moment and gone the next, and maybe she had dreamed it—

Mr. Shardlow sighed, shaking his head as he stepped back and to the side. "You really want to go in there? The French inn equivalent of a deathtrap?"

For just a moment, Beth hesitated. It could not be as bad as all that, surely. She had spent almost two weeks venturing into such places after all, and she had come through that alive and in one piece. Mostly.

She held her chin high as she said, "Of course."

Mr. Shardlow muttered something which could have been a French curse under his breath, then shook his head irritably. "Well, it's your funeral."

And he stomped away into the night.

Beth watched him go with a strange sort of sinking feeling in her stomach. He was a most infuriating man, it was true, and she would not have permitted him to stop her.

But still. There was something about him.

# CHAPTER THREE

*September 31, 1810*

HUGH HAD NOT slept well. He had to assume most people wouldn't if they'd bedded down in a hedgerow.

As his bleary eyes took in the sight of the inn, he wondered if any other gentleman had managed to fall so far from grace. *The Duke of Martock, sleeping in a hedge? A French hedge, no less?*

No wonder his father had been so disappointed in him, if he had foreseen this.

Rubbing weary eyes with a hand, Hugh headed toward the inn with only one thing on his mind. Well. Two.

First, he would have to debase himself and offer to complete some task for food. He couldn't go another day like this with no sustenance. He would find himself not only sleeping in a hedgerow but collapsing under one, unable to keep his feet moving.

And second, he must do his utmost to ensure no one ever found out about this.

*The Duke of Martock, work? Use his hands, for goodness sake?*

Oh, it was degrading, Hugh thought as he pushed open the door and breathed in the sticky fumes of spilled ale.

He would have to hope the innkeeper would not ask him to

clean the place. There appeared to be a fair few people who had spent the night sleeping in their chairs. Even in dark corners, there were people asleep with their heads tipped back, snoring the day away as they—

Hugh stopped dead in his tracks. No. It couldn't be. He was dreaming.

But even after he had raised a hand to his face to rub his eyes once more, blinking several times as though that would provide the clarity he needed, he still saw the same image which had so shocked him mere moments ago.

*That woman.* The woman from last night—the one he had half thought was a dream. So alluring were those lips when she'd been arguing with him.

"Impossible," Hugh breathed.

As though her ears were finely tuned to his voice, the woman glanced up—and they flashed such a look of cold fury he almost took a step back.

No one had ever looked at him like that before. No woman, certainly. Hugh rarely liked using the title or the name Martock, but when it came to many women, it was highly convenient.

There were few women in London who would not lift a skirt for a Martock.

Revulsion rushed through Hugh at the thought. He wasn't that person any more, he told himself firmly. In a way, he'd never been that person to begin with…

But whether or not he used the name, Hugh knew his good looks and relative charm always got his own way, woman or man. He had only survived the last few weeks here in France because of them. Yet this woman could look at him with such…such disdain!

Despite himself, Hugh found his feet meandering toward her. Which was foolish. One only had to take a cursory look at her to see Miss Hoity Toity had no desire to speak to him.

Which didn't explain why he sat at her table.

"You," he said.

*You?* Hugh cringed inwardly at the foolishness. Could he not think of something better than that?

The woman evidently agreed with his unspoken criticism. At least, she raised an eyebrow and said nothing, which was probably all he deserved.

Still, Hugh could not help but try again. There was something about this woman, something that enticed him. Probably the simple fact that she was the first English person he had encountered in weeks, he tried to tell himself. Nothing more impressive than that.

"I thought you'd be gone," he said conversationally, as though they were friends.

Friends! Him, with a woman?

"Your opinion does not interest me," the woman said icily.

Hugh could not help but snap, "What is your name? It seems ridiculous to be arguing with a woman who has no name."

For a moment, he thought she would retort in kind. That she had no wish to speak with him was evident. That she did not owe him the courtesy of her name was also true.

But Hugh found himself hoping desperately she would give him that small favor. Why, he could not tell.

Well, part of him could. Oh, this was ridiculous—it was only because he hadn't bedded someone in a month that he—

"My name is Elizabeth Mead," she said coldly. "You may call me Miss Mead."

Hugh nodded, though why, he also could not tell.

*Elizabeth Mead.* The name did not ring any bells, and the surname was unfamiliar. Not part of society then, the true *ton*, or he would have heard of her.

No, wait. There was something. Was there not a disaster ten years ago or so? A Mead who lost his fortune? Hugh was almost sure—

"And now that you know my name, you can go away," said Miss Mead, far more sugary than her words suggested. "Good day, Mr. Shardlow."

Hugh blinked. Then he remembered he'd been fool enough to give her his true name…at least, part of it. She still had no idea he was a duke.

Which was precisely how things were going to stay, he told himself firmly. Yes, she would probably fawn over him if she knew she was talking to the Duke of Martock. Yes, she would probably give into his attentions and allow him to—

But that wasn't why he was here, Hugh recollected. He was here to give her some advice, advice he would be a cad not to give.

"You are in danger here, you know, Miss Mead," Hugh said quietly, trying to imbue his words with a little gentle reproof.

It did not work. "And I thank you for your opinion, Mr. Shardlow, however unwarranted and unwelcome it is," Miss Mead said quietly. "Good day, Mr. Shardlow."

*This woman!* Hugh did not understand it—he had never met anyone so persistent, so determined to see ill of him. Well, that wasn't quite true. But she didn't know who he was, yet she still treated him like those who did!

Which suggested—his stomach twisted painfully—there was something about him that said he was a rotten egg, even if they did not know he was a Martock. A sobering thought.

"What are you doing here?" Hugh persisted.

It was quite clear Miss Mead wished him to leave, and perhaps that was why she finally answered a straight question. Perhaps she believed he would then depart.

"I am here seeking—I am looking for someone," she said stiffly.

And Hugh's stomach sank. Of course she was.

He had heard of this. He had believed it merely an old wives' tale when in London; it had seemed so fantastical. Surely no woman would be idiotic enough to come to France looking for a lover gone missing in the war!

Yet there were plenty of stories. That was all he had thought them, stories.

Until now. Until he was facing a woman with bold eyes and raven curls searching for her lover in France, to no avail.

Hugh could not explain the jealousy. Yes, she was pretty, and yes, her fiery company was most welcome after so many weeks alone without any good conversation.

But that did not explain the almost territorial desire rushing through him as he examined her, Miss Mead's cheeks flushing at his attention. It didn't explain why he was so jealous of this man she had not named and he had never met. He would have a prior claim to her affections—it was foolish of him to feel so…so angry.

Yet Hugh wished to goodness the man could appear, tell this Miss Mead he no longer had any affection for her, and go away. Leaving her to him…

"You are affronted."

"Yes," Hugh said without thinking, then hastily added, "I mean, not because you are looking for him."

Miss Mead examined him coolly, her dark eyes seeming to grow deeper with each passing moment. "You judge me then, for coming alone."

In truth, he did. It was a brave—or reckless—thing to do. France was no place for a lady at the best of times, and to come during a war, without protection, without even a servant?

*It was madness!*

Whoever had permitted her to do such a thing was playing with fire, Hugh was certain.

And it did not halt the lurch of jealousy making it most difficult to concentrate. He wanted to pull Miss Mead into his arms, tell her this man wasn't coming, that she should accept his attentions…

Hugh swallowed. Perhaps he was the foolish one. He had never been so overtaken by a woman like this before. Parts of him had leapt to attention in the presence of a fine woman, yes, but not his heart.

"And what if you do not find him?" he found himself asking.

Miss Mead's eyes flashed. "I will find him."

Hugh almost smiled. There was such impulsiveness about her. She had not hesitated, even for a moment, to consider she may be unsuccessful. A special type of woman indeed.

The inn door opened and men came in. Some of them Hugh recognized from last night. Perhaps that was what she was hoping; that her lover, perhaps even her betrothed, had been soaking himself in French ale rather than coming back to her. Was that it?

"You don't know—"

"I know my brother," Miss Mead said fiercely. "And I know myself. I know what I will do to find him, and I assure you, Mr. Shardlow, I will find him."

Hugh stared at the pink dots which had appeared on Miss Mead's cheeks as some of his envy started to melt away.

Brother. Ah. Well, that was different.

It was still astonishing that any woman would venture this far into French territory—that she would come to France at all. But at least his pride had been softened by the revelation it was not a lover but a brother she sought.

Miss Mead bit her lip. "I will find him."

It was the first hint of uncertainty she had revealed, and Hugh felt a rush of sympathy.

Oh, she was still being ridiculous. She should make for Calais and take the first boat home.

Still, he could not help but feel for her. Sibling ties were evidently strong. Not that he knew much about it—he had no siblings, and few friends. Being a Martock made that difficult.

Hugh flinched as the memory of the last thing his father had ever said to him rang in his ears. No matter how much he attempted to forget it, he would never be free. Never.

*"You are a Martock, my boy, and that means you'll never be accepted—you'll never be one of them! Society may court you for your title, but you're a Martock and they are not to be trusted. You are not to be trusted."*

Hugh swallowed, hoping Miss Mead hadn't noticed the sudden movement. "Your brother."

She gave a stiff nod. "I will find him."

"I never said you wouldn't," Hugh said fairly, leaning back in his chair.

Her flush deepened. "I know. I just—"

"Want to find him, yes, I rather got that."

*Well, well. What a woman. Reckless, bold, brave to the point of idiocy, and beautiful.*

*Damn.* If only they had met at Almack's—or better, at a gaming hell where he would not have had to worry about asking her father's permission to do as much as look at her. No, he would have been able to pull her into his arms and—

"It's my responsibility to find him, and I will," Miss Mead was saying.

Hugh could not help but ask, "But would not another brother be a more suitable choice?"

She glared, and then her gaze softened. "I have no other brother. Just a sister, who is several years older than me, and married."

*And probably buried in screaming babies,* Hugh thought privately. So that would leave the younger Miss Mead. Fascinating.

"You're horrified, aren't you?" Miss Mead said conversationally, holding his gaze boldly.

Hugh hesitated before responding. He was still growing accustomed to the unhindered way Frenchmen looked at him. No Englishman, knowing his title, would be so unseemly as to look him straight in the eye—but the peasants here had no idea.

Neither did Miss Mead.

"I am a little," he admitted. "But I admire you. You are a brave woman."

The flush on her cheeks increased as Miss Mead dropped her gaze to her hands. "I believe I am rather rash, but I thank you."

It was perhaps the most pleasant exchange they had shared, and Hugh leaned forward. Here was a woman he could appreciate. And any woman he could stomach for more than five minutes together was worth knowing.

"Miss Mead, tell me—"

But Hugh's words were cut off by the innkeeper.

"There y'go, mademoiselle!"

Hugh's mouth started to water. It was impossible for it not to. The delicious scent wafting up from the stew the man had just placed on the table before him was absolutely exquisite.

*Or, it wasn't. It was hard to tell when you haven't eaten in days.*

But the innkeeper did not place the spoon before him. He placed it before Miss Mead. "That'll be a sou, thank you."

"Of course," said Miss Mead with a brief smile. "Here…"

Hugh watched as she revealed on a sleeve a coin purse, carefully tied at her wrist. Ah, that would explain why she'd been so upset at him grabbing her wrist yesterday when—

He almost allowed his mouth to fall open, but he just about managed to hold it together. He was forced to tighten his jaw, though, as Miss Mead opened up the coin purse to reveal not only several gold livres, but what appeared to be a few curled English bank notes.

She took out a sou. "There you go."

The innkeeper received it, bowed, and returned to the bar without a word.

*As well he might,* Hugh thought darkly. Dear lord, the woman was walking about the place with a small fortune attached to her wrist! Did she have any idea how dangerous—?

"I'm starving," Miss Mead stated, picking up the spoon and taking a mouthful. "What were you saying? Mr. Shardlow?"

Hugh started. He had been so distracted by the stew, then the money, that he could hardly recall what he had been saying. Something nonsensical, he'd be bound.

And he had no interest in attempting to resurrect it from his memory either. Not now that a plan was forming—a plan that his father would have approved of, Hugh thought darkly.

That should be enough to tell him it was a terrible plan indeed, but what other choice did he have? No choice at all.

No, it was make this offer or start learning how to peel pota-toes, Hugh thought with a sigh. He'd probably lose a thumb in the process.

"Miss Mead, I have a proposition for you," he began.

Miss Mead looked up sharply. "Have I not made it clear that—?"

"Yes, yes, you want to find your brother," Hugh said hastily, raising a hand to quiet her. "And I am not saying you should not."

Her wary expression was well merited. "Well?"

Hugh swallowed. He had to pitch this precisely right, else she would take fright and demand he leave her. And he probably would. He had a nasty feeling Miss Mead could make him do near anything.

"You wish to find your brother, but you travel alone, without protection," he said slowly as he watched Miss Mead eat, his stomach rumbling. "I wish to return to England, but find myself…short. In coin."

He waited. Surely she would understand his meaning?

Miss Mead looked up. "And?"

"I suggest I help you look for your brother for the next…oh, say, the next month."

She frowned. "Help me?"

He nodded as the chatter of French grew around them. "You are unprotected, Miss Mead, and fain would I permit you to continue unchaperoned."

"And you would help me for nothing?" Miss Mead said with an arched eyebrow.

A lurch in his stomach made Hugh wince, and it was not a rush of hunger. "No. You would pay my passage home, back to England, at the end of the month. It's a fair bargain."

It was the only bargain he could make, Hugh knew, and his heart was in his mouth as he watched her consider it.

Miss Mead had to agree. She simply had to.

She had as much to gain from the suggestion as he did, Hugh reasoned silently. She would benefit from a man about the place.

He could ask questions she could not, go into gaming hells or brothels where she would not.

He glanced once more at the determined Miss Mead. Well. Probably not.

And within a month, he'd be home. Back to where his money was, Hugh thought. Oh, if he'd gotten a note to his butler—but even if he had, the money would have been stolen the moment the letter appeared at the French docks. Confiscating English coin was a specialty of theirs.

Miss Mead was examining him with great suspicion. "You are a stranger to me. Why should I trust you?"

Hugh almost laughed. If she knew he was a duke, she would probably trust him on the spot. It was a tempting thought, but then he would have to reveal his real name, his full name.

Hugh Shardlow, Duke of Martock.

And the moment she heard "Martock," he knew precisely what would happen. She would lean away, make an excuse, and rush from him.

"Do you have any better offers?" he said aloud, gesturing around the inn.

For a moment, just a moment, Miss Mead grinned. Then her face straightened. "No, I suppose not. Why do you want to return to England so badly—why are you here at all?"

Ah. Hugh had rather hoped that question would not arise, but he had been daft to think he could ignore it completely.

Well, he would simply have to fall back on the same old tricks all Martocks used, he thought bitterly. He would have to lie.

"I came to France to help with the war effort, though I did not enlist," he said quietly. "I wish to return to England because…because my sister is due to be confined at any moment, and I am the only family she has."

It was well-pitched, Hugh immediately saw with a twist of his heart. The moment he spoke, Miss Mead's eyes misted and she reached across the table and took his hand.

"Sisters. Sisters are important. She must miss you," she murmured.

Self-loathing filled his heart. How could he lie to a woman like this, a woman who was risking her life to save a sibling? And here he was, lying about a sibling who did not exist, gaining her trust, all to save his own skin.

But her sympathy would be his salvation. And the guilt he felt now would be nothing to the relief he would feel once back on English shores.

"So we are agreed?" he said aloud, pushing away all concerns.

Hugh watched Miss Mead consider. Her eyes darted and she bit her lip. His heart beat faster and faster—

"Agreed," Miss Mead said unexpectedly. "You will help me search for my brother for a month, and then I will send you back to England."

Hugh blinked. "What do you mean send me back? Will you not accompany me?"

It was a heady thought. The two of them, sharing a cabin on a shifting ocean—

"Only if I have found my brother," Miss Mead said, as though it was the most obvious thing in the world. "So, where do we start?"

Jubilation was rushing through Hugh's body. He had done it—and without having to lift a finger to clean a tankard or peel a potato. In a month, he would be back on English shores, all without having to spend a penny.

"We start," Hugh said firmly, catching the eye of the innkeeper, "by ordering me a bowl of stew."

# CHAPTER FOUR

*October 1, 1810*

A VERY SUDDEN, horrible, wet awakening was not precisely what Mr. Shardlow had in mind for the next morning, but he received it nevertheless.

"Ye gods!"

With a great sense of satisfaction, Beth poured a sudden rush of freezing water over him as he slumbered in the room she had purchased for him in the inn.

Beth tried not to smile. It was cruel, really, but it was also a kindness. They needed to get moving, and the man simply wouldn't wake up. After a while, it was simply easier to fall back into the childhood trick she once played on Matthew.

Mr. Shardlow blinked desperately as water dripped down his nose.

Beth stifled a laugh. It was cruel, and if she'd been afforded any joy since she had landed here in France, perhaps this would not have been quite so funny. As it was…

"Good morning," she said cheerfully.

Mr. Shardlow shook his head, spraying water across the room. Beth took a step back and dropped the wooden bucket to the floor. It made a very satisfying clunk.

Finally, she was getting somewhere. After days spent wandering about the place, trying desperately to find her brother, she finally had an ally. Of sorts.

"Good morning?" Mr. Shardlow repeated, shivering as the cold water sank into his skin. "You call this a good morning—being awoken from the depths of dreams by—"

"You were absolutely impossible to awaken; I was running out of ideas on what to do," said Beth in a matter-of-fact tone, as though waking up men was an occupational hazard. "What would you have me do?"

Mr. Shardlow blinked again as he watched her walk over to the window. "You could have poked me."

Beth tried hard not to roll her eyes. Did the man think she was a complete fool? That she had never woken anyone up in her life? That she had no idea there were any options between walking into the room of a sleeping man and dousing him with water?

"I did," she said sharply. "I prodded, I'll have you know. I shouted your name."

"And I...I didn't wake up?"

"Not in the slightest," said Beth, twitching the curtain an inch and peering out the window. "I was of half a mind to merely drag you out of your bed—"

Mr. Shardlow snorted. Well, perhaps Beth didn't look the type who could lift him, let alone drag him—though she was almost sure she could. Gravity would have helped.

"You wouldn't have dared."

She turned to meet his gaze and a flush of heat rushed through her stomach. He really was a most disconcerting man. "Oh, wouldn't I?"

Beth had spoken boldly, but in this moment, she did not feel bold. Here she was, standing in a room alone with a man. A bedchamber, no less. A man who exuded masculinity in the same way a cat exuded dominance.

He was bewildering. He made her feel...strange. Not unpleasant, certainly, but being around him made her feel as though her feet didn't know where they were going.

She was tired, that was all. Determined to find her brother. And they couldn't loiter.

"Well, come on, get up," Beth said briskly, opening up the curtains with a flourish.

Mr. Shardlow winced. "Too bright."

"It's only going to get brighter," she shot back. "And you know what that means?"

The man stared. He really was very damp, Beth saw with a flicker of glee. There was something about doing precisely what ladies were not supposed to do. Something that warmed one's spirits that she probably shouldn't enjoy. *Nancy would certainly not approve*, Beth thought with a stifled laugh. Which was probably why she was so enjoying it.

"What does it mean?" Mr. Shardlow groaned, sitting up.

"It means the day is upon us, and we are late," Beth stated.

There was a strange sort of determined force in her words that surprised even her.

She couldn't just give up, could she? After fighting with her sister to get here in the first place—after the terror they'd shared, experiencing a fight with the Glasshand Gang...

Everything had been to find Matthew and bring him safely home. Just because she hadn't succeeded in two weeks did not mean she would not succeed. And now she had a man on her side.

Not that she needed a man, Beth thought hastily. They were usually a hindrance more than a help, from what she could tell, and this one seemed particularly slow.

But the point was, there were certain places he could go that she...well, not wouldn't. But it would be more difficult. Beth knew she would march into a brothel and drag her brother out by the ear if that was where she found him. She'd just prefer not to.

"Late?" Mr. Shardlow said eagerly, pushing himself up further in the bed. "Late for what?"

Beth stared. Had he lost his wits? "Why, looking for my brother, of course—were you listening to a thing I said last night?"

Mr. Shardlow opened his mouth, and then closed it again.

Beth rolled her eyes. There was no point in attempting to hide her irritation; this wasn't a friend of her family or an acquaintance of her own. There was no possibility she would associate with such a man back in England, and there was no *ton* here to watch them, presume an attachment, and gossip about an impending marriage.

No, for the first time in her life, Beth thought with relish, she could say what she thought, when she thought it, to whoever she wanted.

Being here in France was perturbing. It was upsetting to think that her brother may be injured somewhere, unable to send a message, unaided by anyone.

But she could not deny that being here was very...freeing. "Are you not up yet?"

Mr. Shardlow groaned. "I am soaking wet, woman, rudely awoken and still trying to get my bearings. I am not a morning person!"

Which was an understatement. Beth hadn't been sure that, without the bucket of water so kindly provided by the innkeeper, she could have woken him up if she had tried. The man had been utterly dead to the world—for a horrible moment she had thought he actually had died. His breathing had been so...so shallow.

Well, enough of that. They had to get moving. Every moment wasted here was a moment Matthew was waiting for her.

"I thought you may wish for a change of clothes."

Mr. Shardlow's head shot up. "What's wrong with what I'm wearing now?"

"Other than the fact that you're soaking wet?"

His jaw tightened. "You were the one who—"

"It also stinks, I am afraid to say," Beth said with a grin, meeting his eye boldly and thanking God Nancy wasn't here. "If we are going to continue like this, you'll have to change."

Mr. Shardlow took a deep breath, but for some reason, said nothing.

Beth waited for him to speak. He was a proud man; she had seen that when he had first accosted her. Mr. Shardlow had not considered for a moment that she may not actually wish to be helped. Oh no, he just strode in and did what men do all the time. *Assume.*

Yet there was something about him…perhaps something about the way he held himself. If Beth did not know better, she would have said he was wealthy. He was certainly accustomed to everyone listening to him.

But what was a wealthy Englishman doing in the French countryside penniless?

"And are we going to visit a tailor before we begin our brother hunt?" Mr. Shardlow asked sarcastically, pulling at his shirt that stuck to his chest.

Beth parted her lips to reply, but in that instant, her gaze dropped to the very shirt he was finding so uncomfortable. Her eyes widened. No sound emitted from her.

*Oh. Oh goodness.*

Well, that was a consequence she had not considered. Pouring a bucket of water over the man to awaken him had certainly done the trick, but it had done more. It had made Mr. Shardlow's shirt completely transparent.

Beth swallowed. She had never—every ridge and line of his muscles, and a hint of the dark hair which trailed down, were visible. Mr. Shardlow looked as though he had been carved from marble. He was magnificent. How did a man hide all…all *that* under such a scruffy shirt and waistcoat?

Then Beth realized what she was doing. She was gawping, practically drooling, at the sight of what was essentially a naked man! And the worst of it was, he knew it!

Beth stepped back. "I—"

Mr. Shardlow rose at the same instant. "I need dry clothes—"

"They're on the chair. I bought them from the innkeeper last night," said Beth, averting her eyes and reaching for the door. "I thought something incognito—"

"Fine, right, whatever," muttered Mr. Shardlow, striding to the chair.

Beth did not wait to see what he thought of the clothes. She slipped out of the bedchamber, which she had paid for, and swiftly shut the door.

And leaned against it.

*Oh, goodness.* That was…odd. Something had warmed in her for a moment she had never felt before. It was almost as though—

Beth swallowed. She was not here to find rascals attractive. That was what Mr. Shardlow was, wasn't he?

She could tell by the glint in his eye. The way he swiftly accepted her offer—the man had nothing. What was a man like that doing in France? What did she think she had been doing, staring at his chest like that, like a common harlot?

Just for a moment, Beth closed her eyes. She was not going to fall under his charm, or spell, or whatever it was he was going to try on her, she vowed. She was here for her brother, that was all. She would return to England with Matthew, suffer Nancy's outrage that she had gone at all, and that was it.

She could return to her perfectly normal, perfectly dull, life.

There was sudden movement behind her. Just in time, Beth opened her eyes and stepped away from the door as it opened.

"Will this do?" Mr. Shardlow said gruffly.

Beth nodded without casting a look over the man. What did she care whether he looked good or not? That wasn't what she was here for.

"Breakfast," she said aloud, turning away and walking along the corridor to the stairs.

He followed close behind her. Beth did not need to look to see him. She could feel his presence, her neck prickling at his gaze.

"I hope it's better than that stew," he said as they sat at a table in a corner.

Beth could not help but snort. "You had three bowlfuls of that last night!"

"You would be astonished what a person will do when they are desperate," Mr. Shardlow said darkly. "Or starving."

Beth swallowed her sarcastic retort. Not because it would be unseemly, as her sister would have said—but because there was a strange look in the man's eyes.

Almost as though he had known precisely what he was talking about.

The man's mood did not improve when two bowls of steaming hot porridge was laid before them.

"Is this it?" Mr. Shardlow snapped, nudging his bowl.

Beth glared. "What, warm porridge, with what appears to be a spoonful of honey? You object to honest, warm, and most of all, *free* food?"

Her emphasis on the word "free" caused a shot of what appeared to be embarrassment to rush across the man's face.

"You like this stuff?" Mr. Shardlow asked curtly, though with less fire.

Heat rushed to Beth's cheeks. Like it? It had never been a matter of liking it all those years when there had been no money for anything else. Porridge was cheap, easy to cook, hot, and filling. There'd been a winter when Nancy's meager earnings had stretched to porridge.

Porridge—morning, noon, and night.

One soon learned to hate such a meal. But that did not mean she was ungrateful. She knew her sister had done her best.

Keeping her eyes on Mr. Shardlow and wishing to goodness the man wasn't so handsome—it was most distracting—Beth dipped a spoon in her bowl and raised it to her lips.

"Delicious," she said after swallowing her mouthful.

Then her cheeks burned all the more. Mr. Shardlow had

certainly paid attention—perhaps too much attention. His gaze was still fixed on her lips in a most disturbing way. What was the man playing at?

"Mr. Shardlow?"

"I beg your pardon?" He blinked and met her gaze.

Beth tried to smile, though it was difficult. He was a liability, this one. "My brother."

"What of him?" he asked, taking a mouthful of porridge.

*What—what of him?* It was all she could do to keep ire away. Beth forced herself to hesitate, just for a moment, before she spoke. It would not do to antagonize the man. Not after she had paid for two meals, a bed for the night, and new clothes.

No, he owed her. And she would collect.

"My brother, as I told you last night, is missing," Beth said calmly. At least, as calmly as she could muster. "He was last seen injured, but has not been seen since."

She waited.

Mr. Shardlow shrugged. "So?"

"For goodness sake, man, the bargain was that you help me find my brother!" Beth snapped, hating how swiftly her voice rose. Lowering it yet imbuing every word with anger, she continued. "That was the price for me helping you out of the country, a country, may I add, which is getting more dangerous by the day. You cannot return. You need my help."

"I need your coin," Mr. Shardlow shot back, leaning in his chair with a wry expression. "You don't think I could just take that purse from you and make my own way?"

Beth's heart went cold. Well, that was one option. She had hoped, of course, never to meet with such an unsavory man who would even consider that, but—

"Peace, I would never harm you," said Mr. Shardlow, and Beth was astonished to find gentleness in his voice she had not heard before. "But you are vulnerable, Elizabeth—"

"Miss Mead," Beth cut across with a frown.

No one called her Elizabeth. Not even her parents when they

had lived.

"Whatever," said Mr. Shardlow, waving a hand as though her name was of no import. "My point is, you need me as much as I need you. Now, I said I would help you find your brother. Fine. But you need to give me more information than a presumed location. Where have you looked? Did you write to his officer? Have you tried the hospitals?"

Beth had to admit—and she never would—she was impressed. That was more like it.

It took ten minutes to recount the sorry travails she had made over the last two weeks. Alone, with excellent French but no real idea what she was doing, Beth had found it difficult to make any progress, save to confirm what she and Nancy had already known. Matthew was not with his regiment, and no one seemed to know where he was.

And to his credit, Mr. Shardlow listened patiently and without interrupting. There was nothing that irritated Beth more than a man who wouldn't let her finish a sentence.

"—which brings me to now," she said, shoulders slumping. "Unsure what's next."

It was mortifying to confess, but there was no point in hiding it. Her search for Matthew, which she had been convinced would last only a few days before she triumphantly discovered him, had gone on several times that length, and with no success.

Mr. Shardlow nodded sagely. "Well, there's only one thing I don't really understand."

Beth scraped the last of her porridge from the bowl. "And that is...?"

"Why you are going to all of this trouble in the first place."

She dropped her spoon. "Why I am..."

The man was looking quite calm, as though what he had just asked was a valid question. Why she was looking for Matthew in the first place? Had the man no heart?

"You...well, you astonish me," Beth managed, lungs tight at the mere thought of not searching for her brother. "He is my brother, my family."

Mr. Shardlow nodded, then prompted, "And?"

"And?" Beth repeated.

How did one explain how important a sibling was? It was not something that ever had to be explained, as far as she was concerned. One cared about one's family because they were your family. Without them, you were less, somehow. They completed you. They told you who you were, and you mattered to them just as much as they mattered to you.

Beth examined the man carefully. He did not seem to be jesting. There was no teasing air in his eye, and she was certain if he wanted to, he would. Did he really not understand?

"Family is…everything," Beth managed to say. "Without them, I am nothing."

"Oh," said Mr. Shardlow.

Her curiosity rose. What on earth had happened to this man, who appeared to be so brash and confident that he could not understand the desire to find a missing sibling?

"Well, as far as I'm concerned, family always lets you down," Mr. Shardlow said curtly. "You may find yourself disappointed. This brother of yours may not want to be found."

Beth's mouth fell open. "You—you think he has run away!"

He shrugged. "Plenty of men do it."

"Like you, for example?" she retorted.

It was a cheap shot, but it landed. Beth saw Mr. Shardlow wince, his gaze drop for a moment to his hands, pain etched across his face. The sense of satisfaction she had expected to feel didn't arrive. Instead, Beth only felt guilty. Something must have happened to this Mr. Hugh Shardlow for him to be so cynical.

"I didn't mean," she said awkwardly. "I mean, it's just—"

"I know what you meant," Mr. Shardlow said shortly with a cold smile. "Well, you'd be right. My family…I don't have much of one. I'm here, and you know my price for my help."

Beth swallowed. "I do."

"In that case," he said quietly, "let's get moving."

# CHAPTER FIVE

"WELL, I'M EXHAUSTED," said Hugh, dropping into a chair as his back ached. "Time for food."

"Is that all you can think about, food?" asked Miss Mead sharply as she sat opposite in the brightly lit inn they had discovered, to their relief, just off the main road.

"When I am hungry, yes," Hugh pointed out with a sigh.

It had been a frustrating day. Hours they had spent heading toward a town he'd suggested, stopping off regularly to ask locals if they had seen anyone who in any way matched the description Miss Mead gave of her brother.

"Yes, an Englishman…dark hair…taller than—taller than me? Yes, taller than me. He might have been in uniform, he might…no? No, thank you, have a good day…"

Hugh rubbed at his sore shoulder. He couldn't recall the last time he had walked so far in one day. Walking! Him! A duke of his bloodline should be on a horse!

But he had to accept Miss Mead's purse, though weighty, wouldn't stretch forever.

They had been fortunate to find an inn before the light of the day had truly gone. That was the trouble with this shifting time of the season. Light faded so swiftly, you could be forgiven for thinking God had just snuffed it out.

Hugh glanced up. Miss Mead had caught the eye of a serving maid and held up two fingers. Food would be on its way, which was a small relief. Now that his stomach had started to receive regular meals again, it was putting up an awful fuss if it didn't.

"Well, I suppose that's that," said Miss Mead dully.

Hugh didn't understand. He hadn't said anything, what could she possibly mean?

Then hope sprang in his heart. She had seen the error of her ways, realized it was absolutely impossible to find a man in France. Particularly if he didn't want to be found. Now Hugh was hardly one to cast aspersions, but in his experience, men who didn't return from war were either killed or did not want to return. Neither answer was pleasant.

So had Miss Mead realized that also after another long and fruitless day of searching, and decided to do what he wanted: take them back to England?

"That's that?" Hugh repeated, sitting up straighter.

She nodded sadly. "We may have to start considering paying bribes."

*Bribes? Bribes?*

"What on earth makes you think that?" Hugh asked sharply as two plates covered in roast chicken and a plethora of vegetables were brought over.

Oh, yes, this was more like it! This inn was cleaner too; it didn't stick like the one they had breakfasted in. The rooms would probably be better as well. To sleep in a comfortable bed…

Miss Mead was still talking, but all Hugh knew was that he wanted to curl into bed and go to sleep. When was the last time he had slept in an actual bed?

He would never complain about his mattress at home ever again. His butler had always said he required luxury, but this time in France had almost certainly cured him of that.

His argument had been that, as a man who struggled to get to sleep—and so consequentially struggled to get up in the morning—he needed luxury. It was something his father had seen as further evidence of his sloth. Hugh had argued, as a child and grown man, that if he was able to fall asleep at a reasonable time, he wouldn't have to sleep in until midday.

He had never won that argument.

"—if they do know something but are keeping it to themselves for fear of reprisals, it is not too much to assume that a little coin may grease their palms," Miss Mead finished.

Hugh grinned, he couldn't help himself. "Grease their palms?"

She flushed. "What's wrong with that?"

"Nothing, nothing. It just sounds like you've read a few adventure stories," he pointed out, picking up a fork in eager anticipation.

Miss Mead was still pink. "And so what if I have?"

"Well, the real world isn't like an adventure story."

Why had he spoken like that? Why, all day, had he started to hope it would be his conversation with a French person which led them to this brother of hers?

It was ridiculous. Foolish. He had never cared what a woman thought of him in his life, and had been quite happy to stay that way. So why did impressing Miss Elizabeth Mead suddenly feel so…important?

"You speak as though you have had plenty of adventures yourself," she said quietly.

"Oh, I wouldn't say that," Hugh said expansively, as though he certainly could, but was choosing not to.

Miss Mead's gaze flickered over him, just for a moment then returned to her food.

Hugh's chest deflated. Oh. Well, he had hoped for more than that. If the Duke of Martock had said such a thing at a dining table in London, he would have been inundated with cries and pleas to tell the whole scandalous story.

Miss Mead had looked at him as though he was a rather interesting beetle, and then continued on with her meal.

"I mean," Hugh started again, trying to fill his tone with

grandeur. "I've had some sticky situations of my own in France, you know. Moments when I thought things could end very differently, oh my, yes indeed. But, of course, I was able to extricate myself in time."

He leaned back. Now there was surely not a person alive who would not ask—

"How pleasant for you," Miss Mead said blankly. "And if that had occurred, who from England would have traversed the Channel in search of you?"

Hugh opened his mouth, thought for a moment then closed it again.

Blast the woman. She had to take the wind from his sails.

Because she knew full well there was no one. He had been far too unguarded that morning about his lack of family. Now that he came to think of it, it was rather pathetic that in the six months he had been here, no one had come looking for him.

No friends. No servants. Not even creditors.

Goodness, that was depressing.

Well, there was always a chance this Miss Mead may start to care for him…

Hugh immediately tried to push aside the image of Miss Elizabeth Mead sitting by his bedside, weeping over his inert body, calling out his name. He was being ridiculous. That was a scene more appropriate for the stage, not real life.

"Someone would look for me, I am sure," he said.

But Miss Mead wasn't listening. She had returned to her meal.

Hugh took the chance, the moment afforded, to take a closer look. This Miss Mead had kept up with him all day, something he had not expected, without complaining once. Her feet must ache—his certainly did—yet she made no comment on it.

She was something different. Special, almost.

He had never met a woman like her. Miss Mead had coerced, or at the very least, argued him into helping her for what would end up being a few pounds. Pounds he had in abundance in

England. If not for the situation, he was far more likely to give her money than the other way around.

Hugh swallowed. It was all very well to agree to fleece a woman of a few coins to get back to England. He hadn't really thought, last night when they had made their bargain, about the practicality of actually spending all that time with her.

He rather enjoyed it. No, hated it. It was difficult to make up his mind. Every moment shifted from her smiles to her eye rolls when he did something she did not like.

"You think I am foolish for such an errand, don't you?" Miss Mead said unexpectedly.

Hugh swallowed. "Well..."

*Well, not entirely.*

But essentially, yes. She wanted to find her brother, and she needed a chaperone. He would provide that, and be fed in the meantime. After a month, they would depart together for England on her coin. But where was this brother? Did he actually wish to be found? Or was it a ruse? Was in fact this Miss Mead the man's wife, determined to bring him home?

Oh, Miss Mead had chattered on about this brother of hers yesterday, but he had been far more interested in the three bowls of stew the innkeeper had brought him to pay much attention. Besides, when was the last time he had truly paid attention to a woman? To anyone?

He was the Duke of Martock. The Duke of Martock didn't listen to—

"Are you listening to me?" said Miss Mead with a sharp look.

Hugh tried to smile. "Always, Miss Mead."

She frowned, as though desperately attempting to be offended by his words, but evidently could not. "How long have you been in France, Mr. Shardlow?"

Hugh winced, though tried desperately to hide the movement. It wouldn't do, after all, for Miss Mead to see just how discomforting it was to be addressed in that informal manner.

Chatter rose around them, more evening diners and drinkers

pouring into the place. It was popular. Their conversation would be hidden under the noise.

He tried to smile. "Four months."

Now, why had he lied? He had been in France six months, not four. But that was his way, wasn't it? Always lie, always cheat. His father's way. The way of the Martocks. No wonder they had almost no standing in society.

"I thought you said the other night six months," Miss Mead said shrewdly. "You aren't lying to me, Mr. Shardlow? For I tell you now, I shall take a very dim view of that."

Hugh glared.

This was insupportable! When was the last time a single person had spoken to him like that? With no manners, no grace, no curtseys or bows, no concern for him...

And that was when Hugh tried, desperately, to unclench his jaw.

Well, that was the point, wasn't it? He was far too accustomed to being bowed and scraped to, having every one of his wishes obeyed. It was a rather rude awakening to discover, as he was doing right now, that his presence alone was insufficient to draw respect.

Hugh pushed aside the thought. No, that couldn't be it. It was her. Miss Mead.

"And you have told me the entire truth, have you?" he challenged. "You haven't hidden anything from me? Not revealed anything which may be to your detriment?"

He could see the answer plain on her face. A flush, most becoming, splashed across Miss Mead's face. Her dark eyes were elevated by the contrast.

She had lied about something.

Only then did he permit himself a small smile. Well, that was interesting. Miss Mead may act holier than thou, but she was fallible, just as he was.

"In that case, I suggest we keep our secrets to ourselves and do not attempt to pry into the lives of others," Hugh said sweetly.

"It's not a lie—I haven't lied, not directly," Miss Mead said hastily.

Hugh's stomach lurched. Why did it sound so...so forbidden when she spoke like that? Why did he react to her in such a way that made it difficult to concentrate?

*Focus, man!*

"I merely meant—"

"I know what you meant," said Miss Mead quietly. Now her eyes were focused on his, as though she had decided to ignore his pointed remarks and attempt to remain calm. How could she remain calm when his heart had just painfully skipped a beat?

Hugh raised his hands. "Peace."

She nodded, glanced down, and returned to her meal.

Hugh picked up his fork but found it difficult to concentrate on the meal at hand. Oh, it was delicious: well cooked, well-seasoned, and well-earned after such a tiring and monotonous day. But he could not settle.

Perhaps it was the new attire. The clothes Miss Mead had procured were...French. Hugh picked at the waistcoat with barely concealed disgust. It was bad enough that he was stuck here in the first place—now he had to go about dressed as a Frenchman?

The trouble was, she was right—his old clothes had been the ones he came over from England in, and that had been six months ago. Spending six months in the same clothes, even if the brothels he had visited had a rather spectacular laundry service, had been a tad wearying.

When Hugh had changed, he had left his old clothes on the bed, the only connection he had to the life he had led in England. In a strange way, it was freeing. Leaving it all behind.

The only thing he pulled from his old breeches pocket was the one personal item he still owned. His tinderbox.

"Well, I am exhausted."

Hugh looked up. He had barely noticed his hand had moved into his pocket, playing with the tinderbox secreted in there. "I beg your pardon?"

Miss Mead was smiling. "You beg my pardon? I have to say it is pleasant to see your manners remain unruffled, no matter where you are."

Hugh returned her smile painfully. That was the breeding of a duke, of course. Very hard to kick those habits.

"I have taken two bedchambers, numbers three and four," Miss Mead continued, pointing to a staircase in one corner. "I'll be retiring now. We'll leave early in the morning."

Hugh nodded. "Without a damp wake up call, if you don't mind."

"Then you had better make sure you are up with the sun," she shot back with a grin as she rose. "Good evening, Mr. Shardlow."

For some reason, Hugh's throat went dry. "Good evening, Miss Mead."

Dear God, she was beautiful. And as he watched her meander to the stairs around the tables, Hugh realized that he was not the only one who thought so.

A pair of men near the bar was watching her closely, muttering. With a lurch in Hugh's stomach that had nothing to do with his food, he saw them rise slowly as Miss Mead started up the stairs. They made for the staircase and started to follow her.

Hugh groaned. If he hadn't noticed, he could have finished his meal in peace and then gone to bed with a clear conscience. As it was…

He rose so swiftly his chair fell to the floor, but Hugh paid it no heed. He stepped across the room swiftly, spotting the two men just ahead of him when he reached the corridor. Miss Mead had not yet entered her room. She was standing by the door.

Hugh shook his head ruefully. Loitering. The woman was a walking danger to herself!

Well, there was only one thing to do, and she wouldn't like it.

Stepping forward briskly and aggressively pushing past the two men who did not have Miss Mead's best interests at heart,

Hugh swaggered as though he had drunk two or three bottles of wine. It did not take much imagination.

"There y'are, knew I'd find you here," he slurred in French as Miss Mead looked alarmed at his sudden arrival. "You got the room then? Excellent!"

Miss Mead spluttered. "Mr. S-Shardlow, I—"

"No, I would never keep a whore waiting," expounded Hugh loudly, glancing back at the two men who had halted in their tracks.

"A-A whore?" Miss Mead hissed.

Hugh jerked his gaze to his left. She glanced behind him and her eyes widened.

*A clever woman,* Hugh thought with a prickle of respect. Many women would have needed to have the whole charade explained; in truth, he wasn't sure he'd done that good of a job. But by pretending she was a whore and he a customer, they had shown the two ruffians in no uncertain terms that their "conquest" was otherwise engaged.

"Well you'd...you'd better come in then," said Miss Mead, her cheeks pink.

Hugh saw out of the corner of his eye one of the men step forward. Evidently, he hoped to be Miss Mead's next customer of the evening—the cheek!

And the danger. He had to make it clear he possessed this woman for the night.

"Come here," he said roughly.

Miss Mead did not fight him. As Hugh pulled her into his arms and crushed his lips on hers, her hands did not push him away but rested on his lapels, accepting his kiss mutely.

Well, not completely.

She whimpered. Had he dreamed that? Hugh could hardly tell. He was lost in a sea of delicious sensations he had certainly not expected when he had first started to kiss the priggish, determined young woman who seemed to have no sense of danger whatsoever.

But she was far more malleable in his arms. The kiss deepened, tendrils of pleasure roaring through his body as Hugh's hands pulled her tight.

Oh God, she was wonderful.

And then the kiss ended. Hugh blinked, hardly sure where he was. How long had that lasted—a minute? An hour?

Miss Mead looked similarly dazed, but she had enough foresight to glance over his shoulder. "They're gone."

Hugh blinked. What on earth was she talking about? "Who are?"

Miss Mead glared. "Come in here, just for a moment."

"Why—"

But Hugh wasn't given much of a chance to ask questions. Miss Mead had grabbed his hand, opened the door, and pulled him inside.

The instant she closed the door, she hissed, "Just what do you think you're playing at?"

Hugh frowned. Where was the gratitude? The thanks for saving her from a most unpleasant fate? The praise for thinking so quickly on his feet? Most of all, where was his promise of a second plate of roast chicken, now that he had been forced to abandon his first?

"You could say thank you, you know," he said sharply.

"What, thank you for—for insulting me?" Miss Mead said with pink cheeks.

Hugh took a step forward, raising a pointed finger. "You know as well as I do, if I hadn't made it clear to those men that I owned you for the night—"

"Owned me!"

"Everyone has their price," Hugh said bitterly. Then he collected himself, and shame did twinge his heart. For all he knew, he was the woman's first kiss.

Now there was a thought.

"I did not intend it to happen, but I could think of nothing else," he said quietly. "I am sorry, Beth."

Whether it was what he said, or how he spoke, Hugh did not know, but Miss Mead appeared to be mollified. He certainly hadn't intended to call her by her first name. That had just slipped out.

"Well...thank you, Hugh," she said, more than a little begrudgingly.

The trouble was, the kiss had stirred something in Hugh that he had not expected—but now that it was roused, the beast within him rather wanted to be fed. It was hungry.

His eyes glanced to the bed. "Well, now that I am here—"

"Out, Mr. Shardlow," Miss Mead said firmly, though there was a knowing look in her eye that told him she'd had precisely the same thought. "We resume our search in the morning."

# CHAPTER SIX

*October 2, 1810*

Bᴇᴛʜ ᴛᴏᴏᴋ ᴀ deep breath as they entered the town.

Another day, another town—another set of people to question. What if Matthew had managed to get here and found refuge here?

Her stomach lurched as she and Mr. Shardlow—Hugh, that was—walked down what appeared to be the main street of the town. She could smell baking, hear the crowded shouts of what had to be a market.

*Perfect.* There would be people here from all over. It would be quicker, easier that way to speak to as many as possible. They would find him.

"We'll find him, you know," Hugh said quietly.

Beth glanced over, stomach twisting as he seemed to answer her unspoken question.

For some reason, hearing that from him, of all people, made if far more real. He had hardly been the most supportive of gentlemen when she had first requested his help, after all. Perhaps he could see just how the pressure of trying to find her brother was wearing on her.

"Right, I'll take the left side of the street," Hugh said with a bracing tone. "And you the right. When we get to the market, we'll regroup."

Beth nodded, swallowing all her concerns. *What if Matthew is dead? What if he's not here? What if I never find him?*

Questions like that were hardly going to help, she told herself sternly. All she had to focus on was asking the right questions. The trouble was, it grew so monotonous.

"No, I am sorry, I have not heard of any man like that," said a woman with a flour-covered apron who came out to serve her in the bakery. "And I think I would have seen one if there was; it is a small town here."

Beth nodded, hopelessness growing in her heart. Of course she had not. No one had.

It was the same story at the butcher's next door.

"A man, in English uniform?" The butcher frowned. "A soldier?"

"He could be wearing just normal clothes," Beth added hastily.

It was always awkward, asking a French person if they knew the whereabouts of an Englishman, but it was always worse when the fact that he had been a soldier was raised.

But she had to mention it, didn't she? She couldn't keep that information secret. What if Matthew was wearing his brilliant red uniform? What if that was the detail that found him?

Though her stomach twisted at revealing the detail, it hurt all the more when the butcher shook his head. "No, sorry, mademoiselle. No man like that has come in here."

Beth nodded sadly as she turned to leave. She had never considered herself a particularly downhearted person. It was Nancy who always worried, who saw the dark side of things. Who saw a situation and assumed the worst.

But now, going into her third week of searching, she would have to be a fool not to consider the possibility that he…

"Any joy?"

Beth looked up. She had been standing outside the butcher's, right at the end of the street where the market was being held. Countless stalls spread out before her, some with awnings, some open to the air. There were squawks and grunts of animals, people hawking their wares in French, and many people milling about, filling their wicker baskets.

And before her stood Hugh.

Beth tried to smile. "Nothing. You?"

He shook his head. "Nothing, as I predicted."

Although it was difficult to bite down the retort that she knew full well what Hugh Shardlow thought, Beth managed it. She would not give him the satisfaction.

He was a strange man. Entirely secretive about his past and what had brought him to France, he seemed at one moment to encourage her, and at others, tear down all her spirits.

"Someone has seen Matthew, because he is alive," she said firmly.

She did not miss the flicker of disbelief across Hugh's face. "Of course."

Oh, it was almost worse that he said that if he did not believe it. Beth wished she could put into words how frustrating he was. Could he not just understand?

"You're very cheerful, considering we haven't made any progress."

Beth shot him an irritated look her sister certainly would not have approved of. "We have made progress."

"Oh?" asked Hugh lightly as he started to walk toward the market.

Beth matched his steps, trying to ignore just how long his strides were. She had always considered herself tall, but this man was at least a few inches taller.

"We have ruled things out," she stated, as though that was just as exciting as discovering her brother alive and well. "That is half the battle."

"But it won't win you the war," Hugh pointed out as they reached the first stall.

Beth bit her lip. Then she forced herself from the habit.

The worry churning in her stomach, however, did not disappear. If only it were that simple: decide she no longer cared about her brother, decide it was possible to abandon him to his fate, and disappear off home.

Why, if she could do that, she never would have come here to begin with, would she?

Beth sighed. Matthew was somewhere, and the odds were, it wasn't somewhere pleasant. He could be cold, hungry, lost, in pain. All four, or worse. He could have a fever, have no idea where he was. He could be a prisoner.

How on earth was she supposed to find him?

"Cheer up."

Beth shot an irritated look at the man who appeared far too cheerful, to use his own word. "How can you say that?"

"Because I have absolute faith in the one thing I believe is to your brother's benefit," Hugh said, picking up an apple, examining it, and then placing it back in the bushel.

Beth frowned. As far as she could see, Matthew had very little on his side. He didn't even speak French that well. What had he been thinking, enlisting in the army?

"Oh?" she prompted, as Hugh continued walking languidly and picked up a cheese, sniffed it, made a face, and put it back. "Absolute faith, you say? In what?"

Hugh's gaze rested on her for a moment, and then he continued to look at the wares for sale. "In you."

Beth's cheeks burned.

What a ridiculous thing to say! *He probably only said it,* she told herself firmly, *to antagonize me.* Throw her off balance. Well, she wasn't going to allow herself to think anything of it, even if his words had warmed her heart. Just for a moment.

After all, she was hardly likely to be welcomed home with open arms by Nancy. Not after what she had done…

"You're blushing."

"No I'm not!" Beth said hastily, raising a hand to her cheek.

Bother it all, she was! Her hand came away, fingers warm from her embarrassment, and she tried not to think about the last time she had truly blushed. When Hugh Shardlow had pulled her into his arms and—

No, she was not going to think about it, Beth reminded herself as they walked past a chicken coop absolutely rammed with chickens.

Not going to think about the way the movement had felt so natural.

Not going to think about the confidence of his hands on her waist.

Not going to think about the searing heat which had branded her lips, making it impossible to imagine anyone else kissing her like that...

"What on earth are you thinking about?"

Beth halted in her steps and tried to speak calmly. "Nothing."

"It doesn't look like nothing, it looks like something most pleasant," said Hugh with a knowing look on his face. "If I were to guess—"

"You would be wrong, and that is all we'll say on the matter."

Oh, this man!

"We should ask the people here at the market," she continued, trying desperately to focus both his mind and hers on the task at hand. She was here to find Matthew, not flirt with brigands! "You take that side, I'll go here. When you get to the church, wait for me there."

The tall spire was on the other side of the square and made an excellent meeting place.

Which did not at all explain why Beth felt so entirely strange when Hugh grinned and said, "Fine. I'll meet you at the church."

He strode away before Beth could say more. But then, what could she say? How could she explain why that phrase made her whole body tingle like...like when he had kissed her?

It had been a moment of practicality, she tried to tell herself as she asked the lady selling milk whether she had seen a man about the place who was English. That was all. Hugh had been wise enough to spot those two horrible men—Beth shivered at the thought of what could have occurred—and he had a plan to distract them.

True, there was almost certainly a better plan…

Not that she could think of one at the moment.

"No man like that at all?" she said despondently.

The chandler shook his head. "I am sorry, mademoiselle, I wish I had better news. You search for your husband, I think?"

Beth smiled as she shook her head. Everyone thought that. They could not understand how deeply the Mead siblings cared for each other. "No."

And then her gaze was caught by movement, a tall man with hair that became almost gold in the sun, and her cheeks blazed once more.

The chandler, an older man with a wide-brimmed hat, glanced over his shoulder. He was wearing a most knowing smile as he turned back. "Ah. That man, I think, is your husband."

"Certainly n-not!" Beth spluttered. *The very idea!*

The chandler winked. "Well, maybe he should be."

Beth continued walking along the market stalls rather than attempt to explain to the man just how wrong he was. The thought of her and Hugh married! It was ridiculous!

Heady kisses notwithstanding…

"Anything?" she asked as she approached Hugh standing nonchalantly outside the church.

How did he do that? It wasn't a manly thing; Matthew had never stood like that. It wasn't a gentlemanly thing either. She had met a few gentlemen in her time, and seen far more on the streets of London, and yes, they had a certain confidence. But not like this.

Despite being in a foreign land, wearing clothes purchased for him by a stranger, and with no money on him whatsoever, Beth could see Hugh believed the world was in some way owed to him.

*The arrogance!*

"No luck at all," Hugh said with a shake of his head. "And I have to say, I do not believe a bribe would bring different answers. They have no need to fear us here."

Beth swallowed her disappointment and nodded.

Yes, miles away from the battles as they were, it appeared French life was continuing much as normal. Rather like one of the small markets she had visited in London. Except for the language, it was almost the same.

"Well, we shall just have to keep trying," she said heartily. "Onto the next town."

"Onward," Hugh said without hesitation, turning to take the road out.

As Beth took her place beside him, their paces matching within a few steps, her curiosity swelled once more as he confidently took a right at a crossroads. How did an Englishman like Hugh Shardlow know so much about the French terrain?

Oh, she'd had a broad idea from her schoolgirl days. Poor Miss Pickles, their governess, had worked hard to ensure her three charges had at least a passable knowledge of the major cities in France.

But this was different. Hugh appeared to know all the little towns, even some of the villages. How long had he been in France? Four months? Six? What was the truth? Could such knowledge be gained in that time?

"So tell me," said Beth, suddenly unable to keep her questions to herself. "What brought you to France?"

And because she was watching for it, she spotted it. The sudden tension in his shoulders, the way Hugh's eyes became wary, the bob of his Adam's apple.

He did not want to tell her. Now why could that be?

"Oh, you know," he said vaguely, waving a hand as they strode along a hedgerow.

Beth waited for the man to continue, but he did not. "No, I don't know. That is why I asked you."

Yes, there was definitely something cagey about the way Hugh was looking about him—as though for an escape. But it did not make sense. A gentleman would only come to France at this time for one thing, and that was to join the war.

But Hugh Shardlow, Beth was certain, had never worn a uniform.

"You didn't join the army then?" she asked innocently.

Hugh shot her a look. "Why do you say that?"

"Look, I just want to get to know you," Beth said, which was true. *In a way.* "We will spend weeks searching for Matthew, the least you could do is tell me a little about you."

"You've heard all there is to know. All there is worth knowing," said Hugh wryly. "I'm an English gentleman down on his luck in France, and I want to get home. That's it."

They walked in silence for a few minutes. The sunshine was starting to warm now, but the autumnal season was pulling golden leaves from the trees all around them. It was fortunate indeed that she had decided to come when she did. If she'd waited another few months, it would have been hard going indeed.

"So, you didn't join the army."

"Beth Mead, would you drop it?" Hugh said with a sigh.

But Beth had never been one to simply give up because someone said so. That wasn't how she'd gotten to France in search of her brother, and she wasn't about to start giving up now. Besides, Hugh was hiding something—and she had a good idea what it could be.

"I knew it," she said quietly as they turned a corner.

Hugh frowned. "What?"

"You are a spy, aren't you?" Beth said almost breathlessly. "For the English government. Here in France, I mean, and you were robbed or something, and that's why you're trying to get home!"

It all made sense. In a way, she couldn't see why she'd not spotted it before.

Here he was, Hugh Shardlow—and he had hesitated when he

had given his name, hadn't he? Perhaps it was a false name. His cover name!

Excitement rushed up her spine. Well, she could not have predicted that her sojourn in France would bring her into contact with such an intriguing man! A spy!

Most unfairly, Hugh quickly put a damper on her spirits. "Beth, I am not a spy."

Beth's shoulders drooped. "Oh. Well. You'd have to say that, wouldn't you?"

"Beth Mead—"

"Oh, you can't get around me by saying my name; I am the youngest of three siblings!" Beth said dismissively, waving a hand as her spirits rose. "I cannot believe it. I could not have chosen a better man to help me!"

And though there was no real reason to be cheerful, though they had no additional information on Matthew, Beth could not help but feel better.

A spy, even one down on his luck, was precisely the sort of gentleman perfect for hunting for a missing brother. Why, he would surely know all the tricks of the trade. Ways to get information out of people—he had said, hadn't he, that bribes wouldn't work!

"I understand why you have to be cagey," Beth said in a low, conspiratorial voice. "But you do not have to worry, I won't tell anyone."

Hugh raised a sardonic eyebrow. "I wasn't aware you had anyone to tell."

A little chastened, she said, "Well. The point is, even if I could, I wouldn't."

For some reason, this seemed to antagonize the spy in disguise rather than comfort him. "Drop it, Beth. I don't want to talk about this anymore."

*Of course he didn't,* Beth thought with pleasure as they continued silently along the road. A spy who had been brave, perhaps risked his life for another, would not wish to draw attention to that fact, would he?

Perhaps she had misjudged him. Hugh Shardlow had evidently been weary when she had come across him, but he had attempted to rescue her the moment they met, had he not? Was that not proof positive that he had a good heart, even underneath all the gruffness?

Well, he could keep his secret and she would keep it too, Beth decided. No mention of it to anyone, not even Matthew when they found him.

Perhaps when they got back to England, she mused, she could tell Matthew and Nancy. But no one else.

"Cheer up, Hugh, we'll soon be home in England," she said bracingly, nudging him. Using a gentleman's first name still felt strange, but she was beginning to consider him more "Hugh" than "Mr. Shardlow". Strange how that had happened. Perhaps because of the kiss—

Oh, lord, she'd kissed a spy!

"What is it that you miss about it?" Hugh asked quietly.

"Oh, everything, I suppose," Beth said without giving it much thought. It was England. She missed it all. "What about you?"

It was not exactly a subtle investigation into his past, even Beth would admit, but she couldn't help it. She was looking at Hugh Shardlow with new eyes after discovering his secret.

He was handsome, wasn't he?

"I don't want to talk about my past," Hugh said shortly. "Look, you obviously have a great home to return to, but my family made sure not to make me welcome."

He continued in silence as Beth stared in confusion. No, that wasn't right. Was it?

*"I wish to return to England because…because my sister is due to be confined at any moment, and I am the only family she has."*

"Except…except your sister," she said timidly.

Hugh glanced over, a frown across his face as a cloud drifted over the sun, casting them immediately into a chill. "What do you mean my sister?"

Beth swallowed. There was a strange feeling in her stomach, one of great discomfort.

*"I wish to return to England because…because my sister is due to be confined at any moment, and I am the only family she has."*

That was what he had told her when they had struck their bargain. That he wished to return for his sister—but now he had forgotten his sibling's entire existence?

"You said," she began uncertainly. "You said, you wanted to go back to England because—"

"Oh, my sister, yes, her confinement," Hugh said hastily, a lopsided grin creasing his face. "Goodness, forget my own head if it wasn't screwed on. You see, I could never be a spy."

Beth nodded, though she said nothing.

Well, there were two possible explanations, she thought as they continued along the road in uncomfortable silence.

Either he had truly forgotten about his sister. That felt unlikely, but then, he had been in rather a rough state when she had first found him.

*Or…or it was all part of his cover*, Beth thought with hope sparking in her heart. Of course! A spy would not admit he needed to return to London to report back to his superiors. No, he would make up a story about a sister!

Beth smiled, warmth spreading through her chest as she slipped her hand through Hugh's arm. He really was rather handsome.

He looked at her with surprise. "What's that for?"

"No reason," Beth said, not really understanding it herself. "No reason at all."

# CHAPTER SEVEN

B Y THE TIME they reached a place they could stay for the night—an inn which had seen better days—Hugh was on the edge, exhausted, and wondering just how long he could put up with this. Beautiful woman notwithstanding.

*"You are a spy, aren't you?"*

His shoulder twitched, as though encouraging a fly off his coat.

It was maddening. He had told the truth—at least, most of it. He had denied the lie, at any rate, Hugh told himself, and that should have been enough.

So why did he feel so uncomfortable that Beth Mead believed him to be some sort of spy, or war hero? It was ridiculous. Foolish!

*"Beth, I am not a spy."*

*"Oh. Well. You'd have to say that, wouldn't you?"*

"Almost there," said Beth quietly.

Hugh glanced over and saw the tiredness in her bones. She had pushed herself too hard—*I have pushed her too hard,* he could not help but think. *This day has been long, and entirely unfruit-ful. There was a special kind of tiredness in that.*

Strange. Back in England, he had never done a day's work in his life, unless one counted hunting, which somehow, he did not. But six months here in France…

"Let's hope they have two rooms," Hugh quipped as they stepped up the path to the inn. "Or else we'll be sharing one."

Beth shot him a look. "If you think for one moment I would allow you to—"

"It was a jest, nothing more," he said wearily.

One he probably should not have made. It was pouring all sorts of ideas into his head, ideas he should ignore. Even if he wanted to pull the hopefully unresisting Beth into his arms—

"Hugh? Hugh, can you hear me?"

He blinked. Beth's voice sounded different. She was standing before him in the doorway of the inn, inexplicably not moving. She was also grasping at her wrists in a strange sort of frenzy.

"What's wrong?"

"My purse," Beth whispered, eyes wide as she looked up. "It's gone."

For a moment, Hugh had to carefully parse out her four words to ensure he'd understood.

*"My purse. It's gone."*

But that couldn't be. "I saw you tie it to your wrist, I saw you—"

"Well it's not there any longer!" Beth said, her voice rising in both temperature and pitch as panic overcame her. "I don't understand, I thought it was safely—"

"It must have fallen off," said Hugh, his throat dry.

*Well, hell.* This was the last thing they needed. Now both of them were in the same sorry position he'd been in when they had met—or perhaps worse. He could get by without any sort of protection, even if no one knew he was a duke, but Beth?

Hugh's stomach twisted. A woman, in France, alone, without money?

It was a dangerous place to—

But she wasn't alone, was she? She had him.

For some reason, Hugh's chest puffed out and he glanced around as though he might see the purse lying just behind them. Who knew when the wretched thing had fallen—all that money, it was sod's law that—

"Perhaps someone stole it," Beth whispered, eyes filling with tears. "At the market. I was so busy asking—"

"You would have noticed," said Hugh with far more certainty than he felt.

After all, how would he know? He was just a duke who'd come to France for a little pleasure, bored out of his mind in London, and found himself penniless in the middle of a war. He knew nothing of such things!

But Beth was looking up with such trust, such eagerness, that Hugh's chest tightened. *Oh, blast it all.* She thought him a spy, didn't she? So she would assume—

"If you say I would have noticed, then I would have noticed," Beth said softly, trying yet failing to smile. "But that doesn't change the fact that it's gone."

"And all the money within it, too," groaned Hugh, unable to keep his feelings hidden.

The funds which would have provided a hot meal and a bed to sleep tonight—more, his literal ticket home. Now he would need a new plan. Damn it, and with Beth tagging along.

"What are we going to do?"

Beth took a deep breath, and Hugh was surprised to see that after the initial panic, there was something approaching relative calm on her face. Now that, he had not expected. Since when did misses from goodness-knew-where overcome such a shock?

Even more incredulously, she was now smiling. *Smiling? With this disaster?*

"I don't know what there is to grin about," Hugh snapped, exhaustion finally overwhelming good manners. "We're out here with no money for food or lodgings, the ferry to England—"

"Well, it's a good thing I never keep all my money in one place, I suppose," Beth said with a raised eyebrow.

Hugh stared. "What on earth do you…?"

His voice was unable to continue. That was because, without taking her gaze from his, Beth had slowly reached down her own corset.

Hugh swallowed. Oh, hell, this was all too much. How was he supposed to concentrate with—?

Then his mouth fell open. "A pound note and three livres?"

Beth shrugged. "I wanted to be prepared for all eventualities. I thought, worst case scenario, if I was robbed or I lost the purse—"

"You'd still have money," breathed Hugh.

Darnation, how on earth had this woman reached whatever age she was without being wed? This Beth Mead was far more impressive than any woman he had ever met—why, even half the men.

Hugh shifted on his feet. And it was playing havoc with his body, this visceral reaction he was suffering. He had to get a hold of himself—this was not the time to—

"The trouble is, I don't imagine it will be enough to sustain us for the next month and get all three of us back to England."

Hugh frowned. "All three of us?"

He realized his mistake the moment he had spoken, but that did not prevent him from cringing at the coldness in Beth's eyes.

"You, me, and my brother," she said icily. "Though you are right. Perhaps it will just be the two of us."

Hugh did not need her to state outright that "the two of us" was most certainly Beth and her brother, not Beth and himself. It was plain in her manner, the way she strode into the inn without saying another word.

Still. It was pleasant, just for a moment, to imagine that "the two of us" could be something far more interesting...

The inn was a welcome source of warmth. Hugh had barely noticed he was shivering until he stepped into its yellow glow, standing beside Beth, hovering with clear indecision.

He could see why. That was the trouble with stopping off at any inn that was available. One had no ability to discern whether the place was any good or not.

Hugh almost laughed. God, he would never have thought

like that back in England. He wouldn't have to! Stopping off at inns was something other people did, not dukes. Certainly not the Duke of Martock.

Yet here he was, incognito, and or whatever it was called. Putting up with the rabble.

And goodness, it was a rabble.

"Ah," said Beth weakly.

Hugh nodded. No more needed to be said. The whole place was filled with ruffians and rogues. There appeared to be no tables empty, and though a few only had one man seated, they did not look like the sort of men with whom a lady should converse.

A noise caught Hugh's attention and he looked to the left. He had expected a table of that sort, and there was one empty chair. *Ideal.*

Well, they needed more money. This inn provided the perfect opportunity to earn it.

"Beth," Hugh said in an undertone.

Beth stepped closer, her sudden presence causing a most distracting rush of something through his lungs that Hugh did not care to investigate.

He swallowed. "Give me the money."

Beth's eyes immediately narrowed. "Not on your life."

"We need more, and I can get it for us—I can win it for us," Hugh said urgently in a low voice. "Look just behind me."

He watched the way a curl fell over her eyes as she tilted her head. His stomach lurched. *Now is not the time*, he tried to tell himself. Lord, it would never be the time. Beth was a lady!

Her gaze returned to his. "You intend to take all the money I have in the world, and…gamble it away?"

"I intend to win a great deal more," said Hugh confidently.

Well, it was only a small stream of bad luck that had brought him to the position of no money at all. If those louts had played fair—

"You must be out of your mind," Beth said flatly.

Hugh's jaw clenched. "Believe it or not, I am quite sane, and quite able to win."

*Why did he need to do this so badly?* Oh, it wasn't because they were short on coin, though that was certainly a factor. It was probably, though Hugh was loathe to admit it even to himself, a continuation of this strange desire to…

Well. Impress her.

It was nonsense. Hugh Shardlow, Duke of Martock, always impressed.

He stood a little straighter. Yes, he could not think of a single situation in London when he had not impressed! He was an impressive man. Except…

Hugh's mouth went dry. Except that in all those situations, everyone knew he was a duke. Was it possible—was it in any way possible that the only reason people had been so impressed, so charming, so respectful, was because of the title?

Nothing to do with him, as a man, at all?

"You honestly think you can win?"

Hugh blinked. Beth was still standing before him, and if anything, he thought she was closer. Her voice was certainly lower. She had a mercenary look in her eyes that he liked.

There were layers upon layers of this woman. He wanted to unravel every single one.

"I am sure, as long as they are not cheating," Hugh said. *Well, that was true enough.* "But I think in a place like this, no man would be so foolish."

"Really?" Beth looked unconvinced. "I would have thought people would be more likely to cheat in a place like this."

Hugh grinned. Well, she may not have the manners of a lady, and she may be bold and reckless. She may have entered a war torn country to find a man Hugh was half convinced did not want to be found. But it was moments like this that proved Beth a gentlewoman.

"Quite the opposite," he said quietly. "There are probably so many knives in this place, one would be a fool to even consider cheating. Come on."

"Knives? Hugh—"

But Hugh did not wait to hear what Beth was going to say. It was all going to be platitudes and hesitations, and he didn't want that sort of fear in his mind. If he was going to be bluffing, he needed to be focused. Completely focused.

"Good evening," he said pleasantly to the men at the card table. "May I join you?"

Beth stood by his shoulder, her breathing playing havoc with his concentration.

Hugh blinked. What had the man said? "I beg your pardon?"

A couple of the men laughed. One said, "If you're that easily confused, by all means, pull up a chair!"

Now the whole table was laughing.

"What's wrong?" Beth hissed in his ear. "Why are you being so strange?"

Hugh shuddered as the warmth of her breath tickled his neck. Hell's bells, this was never going to work if she was standing right behind him! In fact, now that he came to think of it, having Beth in his line of sight at all was certainly going to mean he would lose.

*Blast.* He should have thought of this.

"Go and sit at the bar," he muttered.

"I beg your—"

"You, Beth Mead, are a distraction," Hugh said, turning to her and murmuring in her ear, desperately trying not to notice the curve of her shoulder, the swell of her breast. "And if you want me to win anything, I cannot be distracted."

She met his eye for a painful few heartbeats, and Hugh realized he almost lifted a hand to his chest. Dear God, what was this woman doing to him? He'd bedded plenty, but this was the first who'd managed to get his heart racing before the bedchamber.

Beth bit her lip and Hugh almost groaned aloud. Did she have any idea—?

"Fine," she said darkly, glowering as though he'd mortally

injured her. "But hurry up."

Hugh nodded curtly and turned away, not trusting his voice. It would almost certainly be shaking, and the last thing he needed was for her to know it.

He was in enough trouble as it was.

All the men watched him carefully as Hugh lowered himself into the only empty chair.

"So, friends," Hugh said as pleasantly as he could muster. "What are we playing?"

As it turned out, it was a game he had never played before. Well, that could be a setback, Hugh tried to tell himself, but it only meant he wouldn't be making any assumptions. He could enjoy the game as it was, without presuming to—

"Oh, what a shame, you've lost," said the man to his left with a sickly sad smile. "Hand over the coin."

Hugh swallowed. Blast. He really had to focus.

"Who's your lady friend?" the man to his right asked.

Forcing down the instinct to push the man off his chair and punch him in the nose for even considering Beth, Hugh tried to smile. "My...wife."

Well, what was he supposed to say?

"That figures," said the man with a snort. "Only married couples bicker like them. Another hand?"

Hugh nodded, deciding to let the comment go. They couldn't be more wrong, but that did not matter. He had to focus, ensure he won some money back...

After three more hands, he was feeling a little more confident. The small pile of coins before him was significantly bigger than when he had started. He had started off with two, so that wasn't saying much, but still. Progress.

Another ten minutes or so later and one of the men at the table stood with disgust.

"I can't lose anymore," he said plaintively before meandering to the bar.

Hugh tried to calm his breathing. It was all going to plan.

Another few hands…

"Well played, monsieur," he said pleasantly a few minutes later, offering his hand one by one to the final three men he had just cleaned out.

All the money that had been brought to the table was now sitting in a rather glorious pile right before him.

One of the men spat on the floor. "*Merde.*"

And with that, they melted away.

Hugh's shoulders slumped. He had been overly confident telling Beth there was no possibility of cheating—because they certainly thought he had, didn't they?

He hadn't cheated. Oh, unless you counted being very good at spotting a man's tell. The moment he figured it out, it was only a matter of time before he scooped up all his money.

"You did it!" Beth's voice was triumphant.

Hugh immediately pulled her into the seat beside him. "Try to keep your voice down; do you want us thrown out?"

His hiss was low, but there were already many faces turned toward them thanks to Beth's exuberance. Hugh's stomach lurched. They didn't want trouble.

But apparently excitable women were not uncommon. Slowly, one by one, the faces turned back to their games, drinks, or conversation.

Hugh let out a long, slow sigh. "We should have enough now. The only trouble is where to put it."

Despite his best intentions, his gaze was drawn to her corset.

When he looked up, Beth's cheeks were flushed. "Well, I don't know how much room you think I have in there, but—"

"We'll both carry it," Hugh said hastily. The fewer excuses he had to look at Beth's breasts the better. Or worse. He was torn, and that in itself was a problem.

He wasn't here to desire the woman providing him with the chance to return to England. He wasn't here to bed her. If they did end up finding this brother of hers, the man wouldn't thank him for ruining his sister's reputation and taking her innocence.

"Both of us?" Beth said slowly. "Both of us carry the money?"

Hugh shrugged as he gestured to the barkeep for food. He was famished. "Why not?"

"Well, the only reason you agreed to help me was…was because you did not have any money," said Beth, her face falling. "And now you have plenty."

She bit her lip, nerves evidently overwhelming her.

Hugh did not know what made him do it. She was perfectly correct. He could disappear in the morning, fade into the background of other English gentlemen deciding France was altogether too dangerous now, and return to England. He had sufficient coin for a ferry. He may even have enough to get the mail coach back to London.

And Beth Mead would be left alone.

So it was rather surprising, even to himself, when Hugh reached out and took Beth's hand in his own.

"Beth Mead, I made an agreement with you," Hugh said, his voice inexplicably hoarse. "And I intend to carry it out, to the letter. Now, I will go back to London on a ferry, but you will be with me. And, by God, if we can manage it, so will your brother."

It was a rather parsimonious speech. If any of his acquaintances at the Dulverton Club had heard it, a few would have rolled their eyes in disbelief. Others would have simply laughed.

But Hugh found, to his astonishment, that he was in earnest. Though he could abandon her, he would not.

"Truly?" Beth breathed, her fingers tightening around his.

Hugh nodded. "I am a man of my word. And I keep my word."

They sat there, hand in hand, for what felt like an age. Hugh wished it was. It was heady indeed, feeling himself tied to this woman in a way he had never been before. And she looked at him with such—such awe. She was impressed by him. Hugh knew only some of it was based on the truth, but it was enough.

Perhaps if they had been left on their own for a minute longer, Hugh would have given in to the next impulse and leaned forward to kiss her. Oh, how he wanted to taste that sweet fruit once more—

"Here y'go, two bowls of the finest stew," said the innkeeper, banging two bowls before them. Some of the juices overspilled.

Beth released Hugh's hand so swiftly it was as though she had been burned. "Oh!"

"Thank you," said Hugh with a false smile.

The innkeeper nodded and returned to his bar.

Hugh swallowed, but it appeared Beth did not wish to speak. She immediately picked up the spoon in one of the bowls and started to eat.

And perhaps she was right, he thought ruefully as he pulled the other bowl toward him. If they had continued on in that way, who knew what might have happened...

# CHAPTER EIGHT

*October 3, 1810*

**B**ETH COULDN'T EXACTLY put her finger on it, but for some reason, she was smiling.

"What do you have to smile about?" asked Hugh as they left the inn after a disturbed night. "I thought they'd never stop singing!"

He winced, pressing a finger to his temple as they took the road that led, he had told her, to the next town where he thought there may be news.

Beth shrugged, smile undaunted. "The sun is shining. We have money again—"

"We had money to start with."

"Money that we lost," she pointed out, kicking at a stone in her path. "Money we did not have for a time. We are going onto the next town, and I am certain that there…"

Beth's voice trailed away. *Certain.* Certain was a strange word. She had been certain she would find Matthew in Calais. Surely, if he was injured, that was where he would go? Making for Calais would make the most sense.

He had not been there.

She had been certain she would find her brother within a

week. Two, at the most. And here she was, in the third week, with an English gentleman aiding her who she really knew very little about, and no hint of Matthew no matter who they spoke to.

Beth swallowed. "Certain" now felt very different.

"We will find him."

She looked to her left and saw Hugh nodding sagely. "We will?"

"Or we won't," said Hugh with a shrug. "Either way, you should keep hoping."

Beth sighed. "Hope isn't enough."

"But love is," came the unexpected reply.

She stared. Now *that* was not the sort of thing she would expect to come from the mouth of any man, let alone one who had been a spy.

Hugh colored slightly as he met her eye. "What, you think a man like me cannot have a romantic bone in my body?"

"N-No, it's just…well, maybe," said Beth with a laugh as a cart covered in stacks of hay went past. "I didn't consider you someone who would be so…so open to things like that. The power of love."

Something strange tingled in her chest but she attempted to ignore it. She did not mean it like that. She was sure Hugh would understand her meaning.

Hugh snorted. "Just because I haven't experienced love myself doesn't mean I don't believe it exists. I've seen it. Rarely, but I've seen it."

Beth watched him curiously as they continued down the road and turned a corner.

He was guarded. Most men were, she'd always found. Even Matthew had his secrets, those thoughts she'd watched him consider but were never shared. Hugh struck her as the sort of man who had few confidants at all, even between himself and his friends.

But to say so calmly that he had never experienced love?

"Everyone's experienced love at some point," Beth said quietly.

Hugh snorted. "Why do you say that?"

"Well...they have," she said, confusion soaring through her heart. "Even if it is short lived! The love of a parent, perhaps—"

"My mother died giving birth to me, and my father made it abundantly clear he never loved her, or me," Hugh said curtly. He did not look at her as he spoke. "Mine has not been a life of family like yours has, Beth. I don't have a sister out here looking for me."

Beth bit her lip. Perhaps Nancy had been right.

Oh, Nancy was always right. It was one of the most irritating things about having a sister five years older, one who was so clever, so absolute in her certainty about the world.

But she was right about one thing. She, and Nancy, and Matthew? They were fortunate to have each other. And when their parents had lived, they had been excellent parents. Beth was under no illusion that Mama and Papa had loved each other, and all three of their children.

That was just...how it was. The idea that they were in some way special, or unusual, had never occurred to her.

"I suppose your sister would be out here looking for you," she said quietly. "If she was not to be confined."

Hugh laughed darkly as a strange sound started to grow from the horizon. "I doubt it. No, Beth, there isn't anyone who would do for me what you are doing for your brother. But in a way—"

"Matthew," Beth breathed.

Hugh's head jerked around. "What the—"

"Soldiers," she said, heart skipping a beat as she saw what could only be an encampment up ahead. And those were British flags. "They'll know where Matthew is!"

"Beth, wait!"

But Beth had absolutely no intention of waiting. Heart in her mouth, skirts grasped in her hands, she ran forward, chest tightening with every ragged breath as she neared the field.

She had been right. It was an encampment, and those were British flags flying. She did not recognize the troop flag, but what did that matter? They would help, have news!

"Beth, wait—"

"Sir," Beth panted, drawing to a stop by a solider on guard at the edge of the field. "Sir, you are English, are you not?"

"By jove, so are you!" said the man in English. "What the devil are you doing here?"

Beth greatly wished to reply, but she had expended all her breath in running. Footsteps pounded behind her and a hand rested on her shoulder.

"Catch your breath, Beth. I'll ask the questions," said Hugh quietly. "You, sir, what's your name?"

"Corporal Perks, sir," said the soldier, standing to attention.

Beth tried not to smile. It appeared Hugh had been recognized. Why else would the soldier be so polite?

It looked like the same thought had rushed through Hugh's mind, for he colored. "No need to stand on ceremony, old chap. Look, we're looking for a soldier…"

Beth tried to catch her breath, her hands resting on her stomach, as she listened to the conversation. Hugh had evidently paid close attention to everything she had said, for he was able to give the man names, dates, locations, all the details Matthew had shared in his letters.

"—and now the poor man's missing," Hugh finished. "We'd be ever so grateful for any information that—"

"He was at the battle?" interrupted the soldier.

Beth swallowed, mouth dry. "Yes, he's fought valiantly—"

"He's dead."

Beth staggered to the left, all strength in her legs failing. It was only thanks to Hugh's strong arm instantly launching out to catch her that she did not collapse to the ground.

Perhaps she had. The world was certainly spinning, and there was a dull, heavy ache on her chest and she could hardly breathe. It couldn't be true, it just couldn't.

*"He's dead."*

"What do you mean, he's dead?" Hugh asked aggressively.

Corporal Perks raised a hand in a salute. "I mean, I don't know for certain, sir, but I haven't seen anyone survive wounds from any battle, so…"

More words were spoken, but Beth could not take them in. All she could hear was her own breathing. All she could feel was the strong grip of Hugh's hand on her arm.

And then he was leading her away toward a copse of trees, and he was speaking, but Beth could not hear him. Matthew could not be dead! She would not allow it!

"Beth? Beth, say something!"

Beth blinked. Hugh came into view. He looked alarmed, his brows furrowed.

"Beth?" he repeated.

Beth swallowed. "He's not dead. He can't be."

"We knew it was a long shot," he said quietly.

His hands had slipped into hers and she was grateful. Beth clung onto him, heart pounding. She would not allow Matthew to be dead.

"You did your best, Beth," Hugh said softly, and she met his gaze as he continued. "You did more than most, and—"

"I am not giving up just because I have not found him yet," she said, fire blazing in her voice.

How could she? Finding Matthew was the entire reason she had come to France in the first place. It was why she had left that note for Nancy, why she had been determined to get here. Matthew was missing. That was all there was to it, and until Matthew was no longer missing, then she, Beth, would be in France looking for him.

Hugh was still looking at her as though she had just announced her decision to fly to the moon. How could she make him understand?

"You cannot just keep—"

"I will keep looking until I have Matthew before me or a

death certificate in my hands!" Beth said, far bolder than she felt.

Her stomach lurched. The very idea…

No. She would not countenance it. Matthew could not be dead! She would know in her heart, would she not?

Yet her heart appeared to be drastically misbehaving. Why, it was thundering so loudly, she would not have been surprised if Hugh himself could hear it.

He was looking at her with an emotion she did not immediately recognize. *He pities me,* Beth realized with a despondent thought, *because he believes Matthew to be dead. He thinks I am deluding myself. Perhaps I am. But I would never forgive myself if we discovered Matthew had been alive, waiting to be found.*

"We keep looking."

Hugh shook his head slowly. "Until what?"

"I told you, until he is standing—"

"You told me when we made our agreement that we would be seeking him for a month together, then we would get on the ferry back to England," Hugh said, a slightly accusatory tone in his voice. "Was that true?"

Beth bit her lip, then immediately forced herself not to. It was a habit she continuously promised herself she would break, yet whenever under pressure, whenever she felt as though the world was crumbling around her—

Hugh stepped toward her. "Was that true?"

"I…I promised to pay your passage. I said nothing about accompanying—"

"What, so you are going to spend the rest of your life here in France looking for a man you do not even know is alive?" asked Hugh, his brow furrowed. "Matthew would not want you wasting your life, Beth; he would want you to—"

"You don't—how dare you speak as though you know him!" Beth said hotly, fire roaring through her chest. "You don't, you could not possibly—I will find him!"

Those four words rang about the small copse of trees they were standing in.

The two of them stood there, both breathing heavily. It was all foolish, Beth tried to think with a smile. Back home, in London, Nancy was going on with her life as normal. The rest of the world had not stopped merely because Matthew Mead was missing.

Yet her world had. Hugh was right, though she would never admit it. Was her life going to revolve around a man no one had seen for months? How would she ever move forward?

Hugh sighed, shaking his head with compassionate eyes. "I have a great amount of respect for you, Beth, and what you're doing, and I...I like you."

Beth swallowed. "You like me?"

"I mean, you are a pleasant enough woman," Hugh said. *Was that a flush in his cheeks?* "You deserve to—hell, I don't know, marry! Have a family, live a life!"

"If you had gone missing," she said softly, "wouldn't you want me to look for you?"

Immediately, Beth realized her mistake. She had not meant it like that—at least, not entirely. She had meant more that he would want someone who cared for him to seek him. He would want to be missed. He would want to know there was someone out there who loved him enough to risk it all.

It was just, in this moment, Beth rather thought she might. Risk it all for him. Hugh.

He had done so much for her, and had been charming to boot. She'd never had much opportunity to meet gentlemen, converse with them, but she knew instinctively Hugh was unlike most of them. He was unlike anyone she had ever met.

He was flushing. "You would come and look for me?"

"Yes," Beth said softly. "Yes, I would look for you."

And before she knew what she was doing, her instincts had pushed her forward to do what she would never have even considered back home.

Beth stepped forward into Hugh's arms and kissed him hard on the lips.

She had needed him, that moment days ago, and he had been there. She had needed money after being so foolish as to lose her purse, and he had been there. Now she needed his comfort, a comfort that could be expressed in no other way, and by God, he gave it to her.

Beth had thought he would be surprised, and perhaps he was—but that did not stop Hugh from quickly placing his arms around her and tilting her head to deepen the kiss.

And oh, it was wonderful. Beth moaned, the pleasure his tongue was imparting on her almost too much to bear. Opening herself to him like this, kissing him as though the world would end if she did not, it was everything she wanted.

He was everything she wanted.

Hugh evidently wanted more, and she would give it to him. Beth was not sure how, but her back was against a tree and he was trailing kisses from her lips along her jaw to her throat. Beth's legs quivered as ripples of sensuality rushed through her. Hugh knew how to kiss, seemed to know precisely what she wanted.

"Beth," he murmured, his breath warm on her décolletage.

She arched her back against the tree, wanting more even though she could not have explained what she needed, and—and suddenly, Beth realized what she was doing.

"No," she breathed.

In an instant, Hugh was gone. His hands were no longer on her hips, his lips no longer on her collarbone. He had stepped back, hands on his head, breathing heavily through his teeth.

"Christ alive," he muttered.

Beth tried to think, but her pulse was roaring in her ears and she could barely breathe.

Coming to her senses had been the right thing, the only thing to do—but goodness, how she missed him. His absence, the lack of him close to her, was almost painful. There was an ache in her chest that told her only Hugh's touch could heal it—and an ache lower, between her legs.

Beth swallowed. She had permitted her feelings to get away

from her, that was all, she tried to tell herself. He was a handsome man. He was very supportive, very kind. And that was all.

He was a spy, she thought ruefully. He probably seduced women all the time. This was nothing but a game to him, and she was liable to catch feelings.

"It's all the…the heightened emotion, I think," Beth said weakly.

Hugh laughed darkly, turning from her for a moment as though collecting himself. When he turned back, there was a strange look in his eyes that she did not understand.

"That about covers it," Hugh said with a wry shrug. "Heightened emotions."

"Because of—"

"Because you desire me," he said with a charming smile.

Beth swallowed. Desire. It was not something she had ever given much thought to. After her mother's death, the Mead siblings had never gone into society; they could not afford to. It took plenty of coin to keep gowns in fashion, afford a carriage, host dinners.

And so Beth had never spoken to a man like this before. Never had a man speak to her like this. Desire. Did she desire him?

Beth's gaze raked over Hugh, and her stomach lurched. Most definitely.

"No, it's not desire," she said.

Well, she was hardly going to admit to it, was she? No, that would be foolhardy. She still had weeks with this man, weeks in which their connection would only grow stronger.

And affection curled in her chest.

Affection? Beth tried to push it aside, but it was like the wallpaper paste she and Nancy had once made. The more you tried to remove it from your fingers, the more it stuck.

"You desire me," said Hugh quietly. "It's not a crime."

"I'm just confused, that is all," Beth said hastily. The less they spoke of desire, the better. "And emotional. We'll find Matthew, and…and all will be well."

For a moment, Hugh held her gaze and looked as though there was something just on the tip of his tongue. Beth took an unconscious step forward.

"You're telling me that you don't want to kiss me again?" asked Hugh sardonically.

Beth hesitated. She had been raised never to lie, but this was a situation she had never considered. It would be most unladylike to tell the truth: that she would spend the rest of her life aching to be kissed like that by Hugh Shardlow.

Yet she did not want to lie.

"When I want to be kissed again like that," she said quietly, trying to smile, trying to make it clear she was teasing, "you'll be under no illusion, I can promise you that."

Hugh groaned, shaking his head. "God, you don't know what you do to me, Beth."

Oh, she knew precisely what was sparking between them. She felt it too, felt it through her bones. But that did not mean she could do anything about it.

"So," she said, grateful her voice was calm. "On to the next town, shall we?"

# CHAPTER NINE

*October 4, 1810*

"AND I SAID—"

"Hugh, I did not actually ask for your opinion!"

Hugh took a deep breath, stared at the woman before him, and tried to remember how deeply he cared for her.

No—wait. He *didn't* care for her. That was the point. He didn't care for her, he didn't want to kiss her, and he didn't crave every moment to grow deeper in her affections.

*Oh, hell.*

They were standing at a crossroads. The weather was less fine, the sun completely obscured by clouds, and they had been arguing for what felt to Hugh like an hour about the direction they were to travel in next.

It could have been an hour. Or a minute. Hugh was finding, to his great distraction, that it was impossible to tell how time was moving when faced with a Beth Mead, who had absolutely made up her mind and had no compunction in sharing it.

"We need to go further east," she said, tucking a strand of hair behind her ear. "If we want to check every—"

"We need to go west," Hugh said firmly, trying not to think about her hair.

*How did she do it, anyway?* The woman was traveling with no luggage. She had worn the same gown—blue, with hints of lace at the edges, which were getting more ragged with each day. Yet she looked immaculate. Her hair was pinned up. There was even that thread of pearls around her neck. Nestling invitingly right between—

"Hugh, are you listening to me?"

"Absolutely not," said Hugh instinctively. Then his mind caught up with his ears. "I meant—"

"I know what you meant," said Beth with a wry grin. "You weren't listening at all. I think that settles it."

She took a step to the left, but Hugh grabbed her arm then immediately dropped it. He knew what happened when he touched her. Even though Beth had made it perfectly clear yesterday that a repeat of their kisses against a tree was impossible, he couldn't help but hope.

Hope? Who was he? Who was this Hugh Shardlow, Duke of Martock, he could not help but think ruefully, who was hoping?

"Just because I wasn't listening doesn't mean I acquiesce to your wishes," he said sharply.

"You're acquiescing because this is my adventure and my hunt for Matthew."

Was it his imagination, or did her shoulder twitch slightly where he had touched it?

He shouldn't be thinking about that. Hugh dragged a hand through his hair and tried desperately to remember that in a few weeks, he and Beth would never see each other again.

His chest rebelled at the thought, but there it was. He would be getting a ferry to Dover before the cold really set in, and that was an end to it and the pretty woman who tantalizingly looked at him sometimes as though he were the only man in the world...*oh, hell.*

Beth was watching him carefully, wind tugging her curls. "I just think you're wrong."

Hugh tried not to smile. "It's rare that anyone tells me I'm wrong."

"Well in that case, I am glad to be of service," she said with a grin. "It is certainly ill indeed for a man to think he is always right."

Hugh opened his mouth, and then closed it again. Did he always think he was right?

He certainly had been told several times by his father that all his actions were incorrect—but then the old man had been so bitter, Hugh had just assumed the opposite of what his father had said.

It usually saved time.

Was that why he was so definite about everything he did? Hugh could not recall the last time he had second-guessed himself, doubted his decision, and wondered whether he could have taken a different path.

Was that arrogance? The arrogance of a duke? Or was it his own confidence?

Hugh blinked. Beth was watching him closely, but the moment his own gaze sharpened, she looked away, cheeks flushed.

He smiled. She desired him far more than she would admit. He probably shouldn't be surprised. Ladies were not encouraged to think with their hearts, or their desires.

*"You desire me. It's not a crime."*

"I just thought it would make the most sense to head to the coast," Hugh stated. "I would expect your brother to do the same."

Beth's head jerked round. "You truly think so?"

And despite it all, Hugh hesitated.

*Well...no.* If the man was injured, which seemed most likely if he had indeed been in battle, Mead probably wouldn't be able to make good decisions at all. Likely as not, he was holed up somewhere, attempting to recover.

A prickle of guilt seared through his heart as though it were a knife.

Because the truth was, and Hugh was not going to admit it, he wanted to go toward the coast because that was closer to home. Nearer the ferry. Perhaps, if he could get her close to

Calais, he could persuade Beth to give up the search and come back to England with him.

Return to England. Come to his bed.

Hugh's loins lurched. That was the truth, wasn't it? He wanted Beth for himself. He wanted to make her his mistress and never go a week without her. Not a day without her. He wanted to know her completely, claim her loyalty just as he wished to claim her lips.

It was selfish.

Hugh shifted on his feet. "I…"

And he'd never had any trouble being selfish before. Hell, being a duke by definition was selfish. You owned all that land, all that money, the art, the jewels…that wasn't fair, at least when one looked at the world and saw so many poor.

Hugh's eyes had been opened during his sojourn in France. So many poor, and it couldn't just be a French thing. Perhaps if he ventured outside his old haunts in London and on the Martock estate, he'd see the same.

But being selfish when faced with the beauty and…well, goodness of Beth? It was far harder.

He was using her. Hugh knew it, even if Beth didn't. He wasn't a spy, he wasn't a soldier, he wasn't noble.

Well, in a way he was noble. Noble born, but not noble in spirit.

Beth stepped toward him, shaking her head. "You wouldn't suggest something like this unless you really meant it. I know you."

Hugh shivered, hoping she would assume it was the wind. She didn't know him. Not for a second. If she knew he was a Martock, she'd run a mile.

But she didn't have to know.

"But you disagree," he found himself saying.

Beth flushed under the heat of his gaze. "I think there are many places nearby to the east that we have not been to, and I would hate to think I had missed him."

Hugh sighed, turning away as he wrestled with his conscience. If he looked at her, it would be impossible to think clearly. Not that he had been thinking at all from the moment he had seen her…

"Fine," he said with a groan, turning back to her.

Beth's eyes widened. "You—you agree with me?"

"Not in the slightest," said Hugh, his conscience torn but knowing this was the only way he could live with himself. "But that's not the point. This is your adventure, as you say. Your brother. We'll do what you think is best."

And it was all worth it the moment Beth's face broke out into a smile. "I knew I liked you for a reason!"

Hugh's heart skipped a beat. *Hell's bells, he really was in danger here.*

He'd had lovers. What man hadn't? As a duke, it was relatively easy to pay them off when he tired of them. Few women would say no to the gift of one hundred pounds, even if it came with a note explaining she was no longer welcome in his bed.

None had touched his conscience like this. None made him smile as Beth did, humming away to herself as they started to walk along her chosen path. None had ever managed to get him to change his mind…

Still. Hugh wasn't exactly a changed man. "You like me?"

Beth flushed, her pace quickening for a moment. "Did I say that?"

"You did indeed," prodded Hugh with a grin, heart soaring. "And you know, I actually think you might have meant it."

The color of her cheeks was darkening. She resolutely did not look at him. "A slip of the tongue."

"Indeed," said Hugh with a laugh.

His stomach turned over as Beth nudged him with her shoulder, joining in with his laughter yet saying nothing more.

What was there to say? They liked each other.

*"I have a great amount of respect for you, Beth, and what you're doing, and I…I like you."*

There was nothing Hugh could do to stop his face from beaming. It was foolish, yes, but it was a happy kind of foolhardy.

He liked a woman—really liked her. Beth was everything a lady in society shouldn't be: direct, bold, completely reckless. But she was also everything he had ever admired in a woman: beautiful, kind, soft-hearted.

It was a good thing their journey together would be over in a few weeks, Hugh told himself as the road tilted to the right, a row of trees creating a sort of avenue. If it were to go on longer, he might be in real danger of offering—

"What is that sound?" Beth said, halting in her steps.

Hugh stopped. "I don't hear—there."

There was something. Simultaneously, they turned to the left, heads tilting back as they followed the sound.

Hugh's hands curled into fists. "It's—"

"A kitten?" Beth said, turning her head this way and that, as though it would help her see up the tree.

Hugh swallowed. It was just like before.

"I don't think it can get down," said Beth, stepping toward the trunk, her head so tilted she almost tipped over. "What are we—Hugh!"

Hugh threw down his coat and began unbuttoning his cuffs. "This won't take long."

"I didn't—"

"I have to do this, Beth!" Hugh snapped.

He was breathing heavily, hardly aware what he was saying, the certainty of what he needed to do pouring through his chest into his lungs. Because he couldn't walk away—it wasn't possible.

He'd been haunted by nightmares of that moment as a child for years. He had always wondered, if he had been a man, if he had been as big as his father, as loud, as domineering, whether it all could have been different.

He couldn't go back. But he could do something now.

"Hugh, I don't understand," said Beth, clearly bewildered.

Hugh did not reply. If he tried to explain, there was a chance he would stop, and he would never forgive himself.

Living with himself, as it turned out, was far more difficult than he had ever imagined as a child. Perhaps this...this retribution, of a sort, would ease the ache inside.

The tree was cold, the moss upon it damp, but there were enough low branches for Hugh to get a leg up. Once he was in the tree itself, the climb was simple. No one had ever coppiced this oak and there were plenty of footholds.

Hugh stopped for a moment halfway up to the kitten, which was mewing piteously.

"Be careful, Hugh!" came Beth's words from what sounded like a long way away.

And that was when he made the mistake of looking down.

The world spun. Hugh's head twisted, dizziness making him cling to the branch. Oh God, he was going to die. He was going to fall, that would be it...

The kitten mewed again. He managed to open his eyes—when had he closed them?—and saw it had reached out a paw to him, as though willing him to rescue it.

Hugh gritted his jaw. He'd never been one to look for redemption. His father had told him there was no such thing for Martocks; they were just bad men. His father, and his father, and his father...all the generations of Martocks had lied, cheated, and been unfaithful.

"And you," his father had once said with glee, "are no different."

Hugh forced himself to climb up another branch. He was different. He was different, and he was going to prove it...to himself. That was all that mattered.

By the time he had climbed high enough to reach the kitten, Hugh could feel his heart pounding in his chest. Best not to think about how up he was, he thought. *Oh, blow.*

"Come on, little one," he said quietly, raising a hand. "Come on..."

The kitten was soaked through. Goodness knew how long it had been up here, but it came to him quite willingly, crying out wretchedly. Hugh tucked it into his waistcoat, its little head poking out the top by his cravat.

Now he only had to worry about one thing. Getting down.

Hugh tried not to think, only to move. One branch at a time. And now the next one. And yes, the next one did not look entirely solid, but down he went, one more, and one more…

"Oh, Hugh, you were magnificent!" Beth said, running toward him as he finally placed his feet on solid ground.

It was all he could do not to sink to his knees. A fear of heights? Well, it had never seemed to matter. When was he ever going to be that high up?

"He's beautiful," said Beth, reaching out a hand and stroking the little warm body tucked into Hugh's waistcoat.

"How…" Hugh swallowed.

His breath was short, lungs on fire, and the world appeared to be spinning—but for some reason, Beth was in perfect focus.

He tried again after clearing his throat. "How do you know he's a boy?"

*Yes, focus on the cat,* he told himself. *Not the paralyzing fear that almost left you up there, in need of rescue just as much as the moggy. Not the terrible memories roaring through your mind, reminding you that you can never be happy—*

"I was told ginger cats were always toms," said Beth with a wry smile. "I don't know if that's true, it was just something my father always—Hugh, are you quite well?"

Hugh had put a hand out on the tree to steady himself, hating his weakness, hating it was displayed before her. Before the woman he wanted to be strong for—

"Here, let me take him," said Beth, and she slipped the kitten out of his waistcoat.

The little thing curled into the crook of her arm and Hugh smiled, some of the tension leaving his body as he saw it.

He had done it. This time, he had rescued it.

"Do you want to tell me what this is all about?" she asked quietly.

It was on the tip of his tongue to deny anything was wrong in the first place. What, him, admit to anyone—let alone a woman—something that had curdled in his heart for years?

But for some reason, Hugh was saying, "I think I said, once, that I didn't have a family full of love."

Beth's eyes were filled with concern. "Y-Yes. I wanted to ask about that, actually, but…well. It didn't seem appropriate."

Hugh tried to smile. "My father…he was a harsh man."

"Yes, I think most fathers are—"

"Most men were not like my father," Hugh said heavily.

Oh God, every time he thought he'd moved past this, it came back to bite him. When was a man supposed to be free of his father? How many years had to go by before one could live?

"I…can we walk?" he said, letting go of the tree and stepping forward. Every footstep on solid ground was doing him the world of good. "I…I think I can talk better if I'm moving."

Precisely why he thought that, he wasn't sure. Beth nodded and fell into step alongside him.

Hugh swallowed. He had never told anyone this. There had never been anyone to tell. "My father was a cruel man."

"Cruel?"

Hugh nodded. He felt better already. Was this like drawing poison from a wound? At the time, it hurt like hell, but afterward, would it leave a clean injury, ready to heal?

"My father was…he did not wish to have a son who was soft," he admitted. The road ahead of them was empty, for which he was grateful. "I was discouraged from having any friends; even the governess was sent away when it appeared I had any affection for her. The tutor who replaced her did not have her warmth, or her compassion."

Hugh gasped. Beth's hand had slipped into his. At the same moment, the kitten he had rescued mewed happily.

The combination allowed him to continue. "When I was nine, I found a…a kitten."

He glanced at Beth, who smiled. "A ginger tom, I presume."

"You presume correctly," Hugh said with a laugh. "I managed to hide it for—oh, I don't know. A week? It wasn't that long in hindsight, but it felt like a long time when I was that young. A whole week with a creature in the house that seemed pleased to see me. And then…"

Hugh tightened his fingers around Beth's, drawing comfort from her presence. He had to continue. He couldn't just stop there.

"My father found out. How, I don't know. Most of the servants tattled on me; he paid them a shilling each time they reported one of my misdemeanors," he said bitterly. "So they were well-incentivized."

"That's awful!"

"That is what it was like living in my household. The kitten was brought outside—I was made to come too—and the dogs set on it. Oh, they didn't catch it," he added hastily. "The little mite climbed up a tree and the dogs waited at the bottom. I was sent to bed, forbidden from trying to rescue it."

His pulse was roaring in his ears again, but Hugh tried to ignore the *thump, thump, thump.* Or was it her pulse—Beth's? Could he feel her own passion pouring through her veins, thundering against his fingers as she held his hand?

"Your father was a cruel man," she agreed eventually.

Hugh laughed darkly, shaking his head. "Oh, that incident was the least of—I learned swiftly it was easier to have no attachments, show no weakness. I-I always regretted that moment, wished I had crept out of bed in the middle of the night and tried to...but it wouldn't have worked. I couldn't have kept it."

Bitterness rose in his chest. Hugh thought he would be overwhelmed with the memories. Of the sense he had not been quite enough.

"Well, today you did."

Hugh looked at Beth, half surprised to still find her alongside him. The kitten was curled up in her arm, and there was a fierce look of something which could be pride in her expression.

"We'll give the cat to a farm; he'll be an excellent mouser. And remember, you are a far better man than that excuse of a man your father was," she said resolutely. "I hope you know that, Hugh."

Hugh hesitated. "You know, I think...I think I'm starting to."

# CHAPTER TEN

**"I**'M BORED."

Beth rolled her eyes. It was a habit Nancy deplored. She decried the way it made absolutely clear what Beth's thoughts were on a particular subject…or the person they were speaking to.

Once, accidentally, she had permitted herself the expression when discussing something dull with Lady Romeril. Beth had never been allowed to forget it, though she disagreed with her sister on the consequences.

Nancy said it was part of the reason why Lady Romeril never invited them to card parties. Beth said she didn't want to go to Lady Romeril's card parties anyway.

"I saw that!"

"You were meant to," said Beth with a grin. "What, you think you are the only person who finds it tedious walking down miles and miles of road?"

Hugh had the decency to look rattled by her reply. "You are very…direct, aren't you?"

Beth shrugged, pulling her thin pelisse around her as best she could. "I don't see any point in hiding my opinion, that's all."

There was what sounded like a muffled snort from the man beside her.

She glared. "And what was that?"

"Nothing, nothing at all," said Hugh with a grin.

Beth attempted not to smile in return. She was tired, and as Hugh said, bored. The day had worn on slowly. With every hour, she was certain to hear news of Matthew interrupting the same dull conversations.

No, no one had seen a man of that description.

No, no English soldiers had been seen here for months.

Yes, she was more than welcome to buy a little food…

Beth sighed and looked around as they walked steadily onward. If she hadn't known she was in France, she could half believe she was in Kentish countryside. It looked very similar to the fields, woodlands, and little villages she had spotted out of the mail coach window.

She shivered. Not that she would be thinking of that time again.

The fields were similar, harvested now, and the cattle and sheep gathered in small fields as the winter winds grew. The trees were similarly green and gold, some trees almost bare, some looking as though they hardly knew it was autumn at all. Swallows circled overhead then flittered down, snatching at the last of the insects before their journey south.

Beth smiled wistfully. She had only seen swallows once before on a journey to Bath when her mother was still alive. One didn't see birds like that in London.

"What are you thinking about?"

"Swallows," Beth replied before she had time to think about it. As she looked over at her companion, she laughed. "You weren't expecting that, were you?"

"Well no, not really," said Hugh with a lopsided grin.

Beth permitted herself to return it, and then swiftly looked away. She was spending altogether too much time looking at Hugh Shardlow at the moment. And he knew it.

The trouble was, he was a man that drew the eye. His handsome features and strong physique were…*alluring*, Beth thought as her cheeks reddened. Her footsteps crunched the fallen leaves on the path that ran along the road they were following. She tried to focus on them rather than the attractive man walking beside her.

But she couldn't. Because Hugh's lure was more than just his physical looks, it was…his presence, Beth decided. She could think of no other explanation.

There was something about the way he held himself, a nonchalance that told the world he was perfectly comfortable. Nothing seemed to truly faze him.

And that, Beth was discovering, was a very alluring quality indeed.

It wasn't just her who spotted it. Every time they met someone on the road, or meandered through a village or town, she was asking questions about Matthew. So was Hugh.

The women they encountered were far more interested in the man before them than the man she was looking for.

"Beth, I am so bored!"

"Have you never learned to entertain yourself?" Beth asked, amused.

Even when she, Nancy, and Matthew had almost nothing, there was always something they could do to amuse.

Hugh shook his head before pulling a hand through his hair. "You know, I haven't. Believe it or not, I have always had someone or something to entertain me."

Beth snorted. "Of course you have."

He shot her a look, and she realized with surprise that she had spoken aloud. *Oh, bother!* Her tongue was always getting her into trouble with her siblings, but she saw so few other people, it never usually mattered.

But now Hugh was staring as though she had just cursed loudly.

Her cheeks burned. "I just meant—"

"I know what you meant," said Hugh, his voice teasing. "You think I'm a primped up popinjay of a gentleman who has never bothered to have more than five minutes of boredom!"

In truth, Beth did think that. At least, in the main.

"Not entirely," she admitted, cheeks still hot. "I more meant…well. You are, were, a spy. I can't imagine life has been particularly dull."

She watched him closely and was not disappointed by his reaction. Hugh colored, his carefree attitude disappearing immediately. He looked away as though unable to meet her gaze.

What on earth had he done in the king's service? Beth wondered. It was evidently something of which he could not speak. Though she had only known Hugh a few days, she knew him well enough to know if he could boast of it, he would. He was here in France. Right in the middle of the war. So what had he been doing, sharing secret messages? Watching enemy troop movements?

Beth's heart was racing. It was so—so exciting! Far more exciting than staying at home all day while Nancy copied out sheet music for a few shillings a week and Beth did nothing.

"You can't tell me about it, of course," she said lightly.

Hugh gave a bitter laugh. "There's a great deal I can't tell you, Beth."

This only piqued her curiosity. As they walked past a hedgerow absolutely bursting with blackberries—Beth helped herself to a handful—she wondered just what Hugh would do after they found Matthew.

Oh, he evidently wished to get back to England, that much was clear. His sister's confinement would take up a little of his time…but what then?

Would he, Beth thought, her heart skipping a beat, come to London? Come to see her?

"You're thinking of something pleasant," Hugh said into the silence.

Beth looked at her hands, stained by the blackberries, and ate the last one. "Maybe."

Admitting the truth of her thoughts to Hugh felt like a dangerous game.

A game? Now where had that thought come from?

"So how precisely did you become a spy?" Beth asked airily, as though inquiring about his tailor.

Hugh shot her a teasing look. "Who says I am?"

Beth laughed. She felt so...so free with him. There were none of the inhibitions she knew she ought to feel around a gentleman—around any man.

With Hugh, there was just laughter, and teasing. And arguing. She was certain they would find something else to argue about, but arguing with Hugh did not worry her.

She would much rather argue with Hugh than converse with anyone else.

"Fine," she said, gaze darting at some geese flying across the sky in a 'v' formation. "Let's just say, for the sake of argument, that *someone* is a spy. How would they do it?"

For some reason, Hugh was uncomfortable. She could see it in the throb of tension along his jaw, the way he resolutely avoided her gaze.

"Oh, come on, Hugh, it's just a game," she said, and did precisely what her instincts told her without any thought for the consequences.

She slipped her hand through his arm.

The sudden closeness was not something she could have prepared for. It wasn't just that her hand was on his arm. It was the warmth spreading through her fingers, the sense of intimacy having her shoulder alongside his own. It was the way he looked at her, so close now, every sparkle of his eyes magnified.

Beth bit her lip. *Perhaps that had been a mistake.*

Hugh placed his other hand on hers for just a moment. "A game?"

Beth swallowed. *A game.* It sounded so innocent when she said it, but when Hugh did...that man could make anything sound scandalous.

"Y-Yes," she said, hating how her voice quavered at the last moment. "Just say I, for example, wanted to be a spy—"

Hugh snorted. "As though anyone would let you become a spy!"

His immediate dismissal rankled within Beth's heart. She may not be the Mead sister who spoke on and on about women's rights—that was firmly Nancy's purview—but she had listened to her for so long it was impossible not to agree with her.

"What, you think I couldn't do it?"

"I think you would be far too much of a distraction for other spies," said Hugh softly.

Beth's stomach twisted.

*"You, Beth Mead, are a distraction. And if you want me to win anything, I cannot be distracted."*

She had assumed he was jesting at the time. That he merely wished to have the space to play. That he didn't want her breathing over his shoulder as he gambled with her money.

It had never occurred to her that she was, in actuality, a true distraction. What did he mean?

She looked up at Hugh's face and saw just a hint of color along his cheeks. But this was not—this was the sort of thing that happened to other people!

*"I have a great amount of respect for you, Beth, and what you're doing, and I...I like you."*

Beth's heart skipped a beat as she looked swiftly at her shoes, just visible beneath the long skirts of her gown as she walked. This was dangerous territory. Not France, but affection. Desire. Love.

They had already kissed twice. More than twice, on two occasions. What on earth would Nancy say?

"Spies," Beth said firmly. "What does a spy have to be willing to do, do you think? We are just using our imaginations, after all." She gave him a wry grin as Hugh rolled his eyes. "I promise I will not hold you to any of this."

Hugh sighed. For a moment, she thought he would not enter into the spirit of the thing. A chilly autumnal wind rushed through them.

He shook his head ruefully. "There is no changing your mind about anything, is there, once you have set yourself on it?"

"Famous for it," said Beth. "Come on. What must a spy be willing to do? Murder?"

"Oh, I don't think so," Hugh said slowly. "I would imagine—I am guessing, you understand—it would be more like…intercepting letters. Spotting patterns, inconsistencies. Knowing when someone is lying. That sort of thing."

A thrill rushed up Beth's spine. Try as he might, Hugh could not entirely hide his interest in the topic. *And he thinks himself such a good spy,* she could not help but think. *That makes this a double bluff.* No, wait. Was it a triple bluff?

The point was, Hugh thought he was hiding his tracks. Little did he know she was on to him.

"But I suppose if push came to shove, every duke has his price."

Beth looked up. "Every duke?"

"Spy, I mean," Hugh said hastily.

His cheeks were red, and try as she might, Beth could not catch his eye.

Well, that was *interesting.* Although he would never admit it, though he tried to hide the truth, Beth was no fool. She could see through him as though he were a pane of glass.

"You were pretending to be a duke," she said slowly.

Hugh jerked his head. "What did you say?"

"When you were undercover, as a spy," Beth said. Of course, it all made sense! "You were pretending to be a duke—that must have made it easy to get into places other men cannot go. I mean," she added hastily, remembering the premise of their conversation, "if you were a spy. Which you are not."

He held her gaze for a moment. The moment stretched, and suddenly Beth realized they were no longer walking. They were just standing, alongside a French road in the middle of nowhere, a church spire just visible at the peak of the horizon…

Looking at each other.

Beth swallowed. She should probably say something, but what? What could make this moment even better than it already was?

"I…" she breathed.

Hugh's gaze darted to her lips. A rush of warmth cascaded down her chest.

Oh, she wanted him to look at her like that every day for the rest of her life. What a man! What an adventure this was turning out to be. Nancy would be—

A swathe of guilt soared through her heart. Beth dropped both Hugh's gaze and arm.

"Beth?"

"We should keep walking," she said firmly, this time increasing her pace.

Who was getting distracted now? She was supposed to be looking for her brother; she had come to France to find Matthew, and that was all! She wasn't supposed to find her heart…

"What happened just now?" Hugh said, swiftly catching up and matching her speed.

Beth swallowed. "I don't know what you—"

"Yes, you do. We were having a, a moment—"

*A moment!* Beth halted, looked at Hugh, knew there was absolutely nothing she could say, and kept walking.

This was ridiculous, she told herself furiously as desire, anger, and guilt rushed through her veins. She was being ridiculous!

"Beth, what is it?"

She had intended to say nothing. She had not even intended to look at him…but that was rather difficult when Hugh grabbed her arm and twisted her about to face him.

If Beth hadn't been walking so swiftly, perhaps it wouldn't have mattered. As it was, she was walking so fast her momentum barreled her into Hugh's arms. He held her there, and as Beth looked at him, she knew precisely what she wanted to say—

But she couldn't. So she blurted out the first thing that came into her head.

"I'm a thief!"

Hugh's eyes opened wide in shock, and then narrowed. "I...I beg your pardon?"

"Well, not exactly," Beth said, struggling out of Hugh's arms and standing before him, heart pounding.

*Bother.* That certainly made her sound far more nefarious than she truly was...at least, she thought so. Nancy may have a rather different view.

Hugh frowned, and the thought that she could be disappointing him as well only made further pain rush through Beth's chest.

Why did she have this amazing ability to disappoint everyone around her?

"Right, I think we need to go back a step here," said Hugh. "You're not exactly a thief. What does that mean?"

Beth brought her hands together and twisted her fingers. It was so embarrassing, admitting it like this—but the truth had been weighing on her. Perhaps she would feel better if she confessed.

Perhaps then, Hugh would understand.

"I...my sister doesn't know that I am here," Beth said wretchedly. "I stole the money to get here from her, and her husband."

There. It was said.

Hugh took a step backward, as though attempting to see her more clearly. Beth fought the instinct to follow him, to keep him close.

But she had just admitted that she was a criminal, had she not? Why would he want—?

"Is...is that all?"

Beth blinked. "All?"

Of course, he did not know, she thought shamefully. No one could understand if they had not also suffered through poverty. Money, when they had it, was something the three Mead siblings held dearly. It was something to truly be valued, not squandered. The thought of stealing it from another...

And yes, Nancy was well provided for now, Beth thought frantically, wishing she could spill the whole truth out to Hugh. But how could she? Nancy had married a duke! Surely there were far stricter penalties for those who stole from nobility?

"All I heard is that you *borrowed* some money from your sister to find your brother," Hugh said slowly, that lopsided smile of his returning. "From everything you have said, I would imagine your sister—Nancy, isn't it?"

Beth nodded.

"I would imagine Nancy may not like the secrecy of your…expedition," said Hugh with a laugh. "But I cannot imagine she would disagree with your aim. I do not think you need to castigate yourself for that, Beth. You…you are a good person. Far better than I."

Why was there such bitterness in his voice?

Beth's breath was caught in her lungs, every moment a challenge. Not until now had she realized just what a weight her theft had caused. Her shoulders felt lighter, that twinge in her neck was gone, and she wanted to embrace Hugh and—

She managed to stop herself just before she stepped forward. They had proven themselves unable to control their desires when they embraced, Beth reminded herself with flaming cheeks. It was probably a good idea not to tempt fate again.

"You know, I don't think anyone knows me better now than you," Beth said softly. "Even my sister didn't expect me to…well. I left a note. But it would have been a surprise."

Hugh's gaze burned into hers. "I rather like that."

"Except for Matthew, of course," Beth added, unable to explain why his look made her feel so…so warm. "My brother."

"And I," said Hugh with a growl, "am not your brother."

Beth attempted to avoid his eye as she strode past him and onward, toward the spire, toward another village to find Matthew. "I-I know that."

# CHAPTER ELEVEN

*October 5, 1810*

HUGH GRITTED HIS teeth. "Absolutely not."

The woman was insufferable! Every time he thought he could feel nothing but admiration and adoration for her—

"You know, I'm hearing that a lot at the moment," said Beth sweetly. "And yet, you know, I don't recall asking for your opinion?"

Hugh's jaw was starting to ache. "I just think—"

"I did not ask for your opinion, or what you think, or anything like that," Beth said decidedly, jutting out her chin. "And that's final."

"Lord's sake, woman!" Hugh exploded, turning away and bringing his hands to his head.

What on earth had he done in life to deserve this? Stick him with a woman, fine. A woman with money, a woman who could take him home. Perfect. So why did she have to be such a…so incredibly…

Hugh tried to take a deep breath and not to look to his left, where he would see what had precipitated the argument in the first place.

It was a mistake. Worse, it could be a deadly mistake. The

very last thing they should do is what Beth Mead had just suggested, and it was maddening she could not see that!

So instead, they were standing here in a lane, about a mile from where she wanted to go, arguing about it.

Hugh's chest was tight, every breath a struggle. When they had arrived here in this little town late last night, he had thought their luck had finally been turning. There had been chatter at the inn about Englishmen taken prisoner. Beth's ears had pricked up and before he could stop her, she had barreled off to speak to them.

Even then, he hadn't thought she would be this foolish.

"Beth, I think you need to slow down," Hugh said in as calm a voice as possible, turning back to her. His stomach lurched. Why were the irritating ones always the pretty ones? "If you even think about going over there—"

"I didn't ask you!" Beth said haughtily. "I do not require you to come with me—"

"If you think I am just going to watch you march over there, to a French encampment of soldiers, then you don't know me at all!" Hugh said tersely.

His heart ached at the very thought. Dear God, the danger she would be in!

Despite himself, Hugh could not prevent his gaze shifting to the field in question. There, high on the hill, flags flying, was a mass of blue and white uniforms. Tents, the smoke of fires, and just out of hearing but somehow felt through the body, the steady beat of a drum.

Hugh swallowed. It was infuriating. Yes, fine, there was a possibility Matthew Mead was one of the unfortunate men taken prisoner over there.

He shivered. *Poor devil.*

But that did not mean his sister could just—

"I'll pay you."

Hugh blinked. Beth came into focus, her expression desperate, fingers scrabbling down the front of her corset.

"Oh, hang on," he said weakly.

"You'll need money won't you, when we get back to England?" Beth said, her voice tight with panic. "I can give you money—"

"My opinions cannot be bought," Hugh muttered.

Dear God, the woman was beyond desperate. She was despairing. But that did not mean he could happily watch her approach French soldiers and beg for their assistance. Did she have no comprehension of how dangerous that would be? Could she not understand—

"Every man has his price," Beth said darkly. "You told me that, didn't you?"

Hugh opened his mouth, hesitated, and then closed it again.

Blast her, she was right. At least, he had almost said that, his treacherous tongue accidentally revealing himself...

*"Every duke has his price..."*

He had managed to cover up the mistake relatively well. He wasn't sure how he would have explained to Beth that he was secretly a duke. Allowing her to continue to believe the falsehood that he was a spy was weighing heavily enough on his conscience. But this?

Beth was eying him curiously. "Why are you being so...so strange about this?"

Hugh's stomach lurched. "Because...because I feel protective of you."

It was perhaps the wrong thing to say, but he couldn't think of any other explanation. And it was the truth, something he was unaccustomed to telling.

He had to protect her. The idea of something happening to Beth, the one woman he had ever spent copious amounts of time with and not loathed her by the end of it...it was abhorrent.

"I just want to keep you safe," he said, hating how plaintive his voice sounded. He cleared his throat. "As I would do for any young lady, any English lady, in distress."

Was that sudden disappointment across her face? A dip of her chin, a bite of her lip?

Hugh had noticed her do that several times, but there never seemed to be much rhyme or reason for it. Disappointment? Frustration? Embarrassment? Whatever it was, he had to make her understand—even if she may wish to march on ahead, she had to see.

"Beth, we are outnumbered," Hugh said softly, throwing out his arms. "There's a whole army out there, and we are just two people."

Beth swallowed. "Right is on our side."

"I don't care who wins this war—"

"I mean, it is right to try and find my brother," she said, interrupting him with a soft voice that would brook no opposition. "And even if Matthew isn't there, someone is. There are men there, Englishmen, whose loved ones may not know they are still alive. We could—I don't know, take messages back to England..."

And this, Hugh realized with an unpleasant start in his stomach, was why he liked her so much. Beth Mead had a missing brother, yet she still thought of how she could help others.

Oh, hang it all.

"Fine," he said wearily.

Beth perked up. "I beg your—"

"You heard me, come on," Hugh said, shaking his head. "We'd better get over there and away as quickly as possible. And may God forgive me."

It was worth it, even before they arrived at the encampment, just to see the smile on her face. *Oh, hell,* Hugh thought wretchedly as they left the lane and started tramping over the muddy field. Wet boots, damp breeches, and he was falling in love...

The soldier stationed on guard looked suspicious as they approached.

*As well he might,* Hugh thought. If he was stationed to alert a whole regiment of soldiers about danger, a woman and a man approaching would look very suspicious indeed.

"Hold!" the soldier barked in French. "Who goes?"

Hugh glanced at Beth, who appeared a little dismayed but resolute.

"My name is Elizabeth Mead," she began, "and—"

"Brothel is to the left," snapped the soldier. "On your way—"

"How dare you! I will have you know, I am a lady of good repute. I would never—"

"I think I'll take it from here," Hugh said hastily, stepping protectively between the berating woman and the astonished soldier.

Not to protect her, of course. Beth did not need anyone to protect her. It was more the soldier he was worried about—Beth looked as though she was about to launch herself forward and attack him. Honestly, he didn't fancy the soldier's chances.

"She should be locked up!" the solider muttered in French. "Outrageous, how she—"

"We have come about the English prisoners," Hugh said. "We were told they would be ready for us."

He could almost feel Beth's surprise behind him, and hoped to goodness the soldier did not look too closely.

It was a gamble, that was for sure. But he had found just marching into a place and demanding what you wanted tended to get you precisely that. What you wanted.

Perhaps it was a habit he had gained as a duke. Perhaps wealth, nobility, a certain type of upbringing permitted one to march about the place and always get your way. Hugh wasn't sure. What he did know was that the soldier looked disconcerted about being spoken to like that, and that was precisely how he wanted him.

"Come on, come on, I haven't got all day," said Hugh, allowing irritation to seep through into his words. "Where are they, man?"

"They—we were not told—five tents along," stammered the unfortunate soldier.

Hugh nodded curtly, as he imagined a spy may do. You

know, this wasn't half bad, once you got used to it. After no privileges as a duke for the last six months in France, it was rather pleasant to have someone immediately snap to attention and obey your every whim.

"Well come on, show us the way," Hugh said fiercely.

Beth stayed close to his side as they walked slowly into the French camp. If she was anything like him, her heart would be hammering. This was dangerous, foolish, even for him. He may not care what happened to him, but the thought of one of these men hurting Beth…

Curious eyes followed them as they trailed after the solider taking them to the tent. Hugh ensured to keep his back straight, head up, and exude that nonchalance his father had demanded he portray.

"The world should know you're a duke, even if you haven't been introduced," he would always say. "The world is watching."

And by God, didn't he feel it? By the time they reached the tent in question and were ushered in, Hugh was relieved. He wasn't entirely sure how much longer he could do that.

There were three men, all in various states of injury, in the tent. Hugh saw Beth's eyes widen, dart about, and then close in unspoken misery.

His heart sank. *Matthew Mead was not here.*

"That will be all," he snapped at the French guard.

"But—"

"I said that will be all!"

Hugh waited just two heartbeats after he'd gone to rush to Beth's side. "Beth—"

"He's not here," she said, drawing a deep, ragged breath. "But that just means he is somewhere else. I will find him."

Damn, she was impressive. Hugh hardly knew what to do with himself—comfort her? How? She appeared to have taken the absence of her brother to heart, then immediately regrouped and made her next determination.

Which, unfortunately for Hugh, appeared to involve him.

"We'll take them with us."

Hugh blinked. "We absolutely will n—"

"Get ready, men, we're breaking you out of here," Beth said cheerfully. "Gather all your belongings and—"

"Beth!" Hugh hissed, grabbing her arm and pulling her aside, chest tightening. What in blazes was she playing at?

She looked up, all innocent eyes and rosebud mouth. "Well we can't leave them—"

"This is a tent, woman, not a wall," Hugh said in a dark undertone. "You cannot just announce an escape! Did you not give a moment's thought to the fact we are being spied on?"

Beth appeared about to retort, but some of the fire left her eyes. "Ah."

"Ah, indeed." Hugh shook his head. There was much to admire about this woman, and he was learning new reasons with every passing day. But subtle, she was not.

"But Hugh—"

"Stand here, and be quiet," he demanded.

Striding toward the three Englishmen who looked completely bewildered, Hugh tried desperately to think.

He had managed to talk his way into here. He was almost certain he could talk himself and Beth out—after all, they were not in the uniform of English soldiers. But encouraging a regiment to release three prisoners? They weren't just outnumbered. They were outgunned.

Hugh's stomach twisted, fingers clenching momentarily into fists. "If we can leave, we should," he said in an undertone to the three men. "You can all walk?"

They nodded.

One said quietly, "I had no idea English spies were—"

"Are you ready to leave right now?" Hugh cut across him, glancing at Beth. That was all he needed, for that falsehood to be confirmed in her hearing. "Right. Let's go."

*Confidence*, he told himself as he pulled back the tent flap for Beth and her three English rescues—soldiers. That was what he needed. To demonstrate so much confidence, it was almost impossible to question.

Hugh swallowed. If that were possible.

Striding onward, he kept his eyes forward and did not bother to look at the French soldiers on either side of them as though they were so below his notice, he hardly saw them.

And it almost worked, too. In fact, the five of them had managed to reach the very edge of the perimeter where the guard solider they had already spoken to was still standing. The three soldiers marched past him without looking back.

The tension in Hugh's chest started to melt away. Well, they may not have found Matthew Mead, but they had at least done something. Now all he had to do was—

"I still think there is room for you in the brothel, monsieur," leered the French soldier. "If you ever get tired of that one."

For a moment, Hugh had no idea who the man was talking to. Then he noticed the pointed stare, right at him.

And fury, real fury, the like of which he had never known before, burst out of his heart and flooded his veins. That anyone could talk about Beth like that—the woman had been insulted and he would not stand for it!

"Hugh—"

She put a hand on his arm, but Hugh swiftly shrugged it off. The English soldiers had broken into a run, they were almost at the hedgerow, and no one seemed to be after them. That meant he could do what he liked.

"You cur!" Hugh spat through gritted teeth, lunging at the Frenchman.

The thing was, he wasn't getting very far. For an instant, Hugh could not understand why—then he registered the weight on his back, the hands around his chest.

"Hugh, no!"

"Oh, you think you wish to defend your pretty lady?" scoffed the French solider. "Why do you come here, eh? Taking away our prisoners, flaunting your woman—"

Hugh roared, words utterly lost, just anger pouring from his lips.

But Beth was stronger than expected. Her sheer weight was preventing him from advancing, and though Hugh would dearly love to punch the idiot on the nose, he could see out of the corner of his eye a few other French soldiers running over, eager to see the cause of all the noise.

Swallowing bitter bile, hating he was unable to do anything but conscious he had Beth to think about, Hugh tried to take a deep breath. His head was pounding, pain shooting across his temples, but he couldn't stay.

He had to walk away.

Every single step cost him. Beth was no longer hanging onto him, instead half walking, half running alongside him. They strode away in silence, though even if she had spoken, all Hugh could hear was pounding in his ears.

Only when they had once again reached the lane—the English soldiers now completely gone from view—did Hugh stop and lean against what appeared to be the wall of a barn. The cool of the stone started to return him to his wits.

Dear God, that had been close.

"Hugh, what were you thinking?" Beth breathed.

Hugh's heart lurched. Hang it, he was falling in love. And with a woman of no title, nor fortune, nothing. No connections, no betterment for the Martock name. Real danger.

Oh, and there was also that little problem of being in France, in a war torn country, looking for a man who was probably dead.

Hugh swallowed. Not that he could say any of that. "I wasn't."

"I should think not!" Beth seemed as breathless as he felt. "What would you have done if there had been real trouble?"

"Real—woman, what do you call that?" Hugh asked, jabbing a finger in the direction of the field. "As opposed to the enjoyable trouble we had back there?"

Real trouble? He didn't know what sort of life Beth Mead led in London, but if this was any indication, she associated with some dangerous people!

"I couldn't," he said, his breathing starting to slow. "I wouldn't have let—I would have gotten a hold of myself."

*Eventually*, Hugh thought, but he wasn't foolish enough to say that aloud.

It had been years since he had really lost his temper. Even then, it had been as a very young man. Untested, untried in the world, desperate to prove himself as more than a Martock.

Even though he hadn't.

But he'd never had someone like Beth to defend.

His head was spinning, and Hugh knew he'd never forget that moment of immediate decision. When he didn't have to consider what to do, it had been obvious. He had to keep Beth safe, at any cost. Even if that had meant his own detriment.

Even, and Hugh hardly knew where this thought was coming from, but knew it could not be denied, if it cost his own life.

"I will keep you safe," Hugh said quietly. "I said, didn't I? When we made our agreement, that I would act as your chaperone."

"I think I have acted more as yours," Beth said with a weak smile.

He could see the fear in her and he hated himself for causing it. True, it had been her idea to go to the French camp, but he had been the one to march in, then pick a fight with a guard because he was goaded into it.

Beth watched him closely. "What would you have done, I wonder, to protect me?"

Hugh swallowed. "Anything."

The flush on her cheeks matched the color in his own. Hugh knew from this moment on, there would be no point in attempting to pretend, to themselves or each other, that there wasn't something between them.

All he had to do was not act on it.

# CHAPTER TWELVE

*October 6, 1810*

BETH HAD NOT slept well. The inn they had managed to find last night had been more a house with two spare rooms—thank goodness there were two—and the bed in her chamber had been most inadequate.

Still. Her tiredness did not explain why she was seeing things.

"It's a horse," she said blankly.

Hugh grinned as he stretched out his hands to the tall beast alongside him. "Tada!"

Beth blinked. It was a particularly dull, gray day. It had rained heavily in the night, the road coated in mud. And there, standing beside Hugh, was…a horse.

"It's a horse," she said again, as though that would in any way explain it.

Hugh nodded. "I was fortunate, actually. The man selling him was about to take him to market, but I told him we'd take him for a very fine price."

Beth's stomach lurched. "Price?"

A man dressed as a farmer appeared from the other side of the horse. *My word*, Beth thought hurriedly, taking a step back. The horse was really very tall. How else could a man hide behind it?

"Yes, price," said the man with a smile. "Your husband here—"

Beth shot Hugh a look. He shrugged with that non-apologetic smile she was beginning to find quite charming. *Trust Hugh to use that old excuse.*

"—told me you would be happy to pay," continued the farmer. "And such a reasonable price too."

Beth caught Hugh's gaze. He wilted under the ferocity of her look and stepped over to her, lowering his voice as he glanced at the farmer.

"It really is a good price," he said quietly.

"What on earth do you know about the price of horses?" Beth breathed.

It could have been her imagination, but for some reason, Hugh did not appear to wish to meet her gaze. "Oh, you know. I've bought a few. Here and there."

*A few horses, here or there?* Beth tried to comprehend what Hugh was telling her. Was this something to do with being a spy? Had he been required to source his own steeds?

That still didn't explain why he was unwilling to look at her. "Hugh."

"Hmmm?" he said nonchalantly, finally meeting her gaze.

Beth raised an eyebrow. "What are you not telling me?"

"You're a very suspicious woman, you know that?" he said, folding his arms.

Tempting as it was to smile, Beth forced herself to remain stern. That was what Nancy would have done, and people told Nancy things. They confessed.

Hugh sighed. "Fine. The price is a little high—"

"Hugh Shardlow!"

"—almost all the money we have, actually," he continued, his words speeding up rapidly as he raised a hand to placate her. "But I've thought it all through!"

Beth shook her head ruefully. "You have, have you?"

It was most irritating.

Oh, not what Hugh had done. A bargain had been struck, and it was not in her nature to ignore a bargain. Besides, even Beth could see the merits of having a horse. They would cover a great deal more ground than on foot. They would find Matthew more swiftly.

But honestly, almost all the money they had?

"What about the ship home?" Beth said darkly. "I suppose you didn't consider that."

"In fact, I have," said Hugh with a charming smile. "We will hardly wish to take the horse to England with us. To be honest, I think it'll be difficult to find a ship to take him. So we sell him, there and then. Ports always need horses. Then we'll have the money for our fare."

Beth bit her lip. It wasn't the worst plan she had ever heard. "Hmmm."

"And isn't he a magnificent beast?" Hugh said in a wheedling tone, looking at the horse then back to her.

Beth rolled her eyes. "We are not in the market for a horse!"

"Beth, I shook on it. A gentleman never goes back on his word." Hugh gave a lopsided grin.

Well, it was a complete fait accompli. No wonder the man had lurched out of his chair and out of the inn when the horse walked past the window. She had thought that odd at the time, but now she knew it was entirely Hugh's plan.

And though she would not admit it, her feet were sore. All this walking!

"A gentleman shouldn't buy horses with other people's money," she pointed out.

Hugh grinned. "Whoops."

Fine," Beth said begrudgingly, throwing up her hands. "We'll buy the horse."

"Zeus."

She could not help it now. She laughed. "You are not going to name him—"

"I always name my horses after gods. What can I say? It is a foible of mine," said Hugh, eyes glittering with mischief. "Right, hand over the money. I'll settle up with our friend here."

Beth leaned against the inn as she watched Hugh haggle in French, attempting to retain every last sou. It was to no avail. Hugh had shaken on a price; that was the price.

Still. It was always worth trying.

What caught her eye was the way Hugh did it. Not in a highhanded manner, not exactly, but…well. As though the man owed him something. As though it were an honor merely to be doing business with Hugh at all. It was not the only strange thing about him. Hugh Shardlow had all the makings of a gentleman, Beth mused, yet all the street smarts of a man who had lived by his wits for a long time.

Which made sense, of course, Hugh being a spy, she reminded herself. One day, she would hear all about it.

"Well, there we are!" said Hugh proudly, shaking hands with the man. "You are the proud owner of a horse. Come and say hello to Zeus."

Beth did not walk over to the beast.

Hugh glanced over his shoulder. "Come on!"

Perhaps she should have mentioned it before the haggling, and the handshake, and the exchange of money. But a small part of her hadn't quite believed he was actually going to do it.

And now it was too late. She'd have to admit it.

"But I…well, I've never ridden a horse," Beth said weakly.

Hugh looked astonished. "Never ridden a horse? Whyever not?"

She chuckled, shaking her head as she nervously approached the large animal. "Only a man who has grown up with money would ask that."

A flicker of disconcertion darkened Hugh's face, but it was gone in an instant. "Oh."

"Oh indeed," said Beth wryly. "I suppose you did not think to barter for, oh, I don't know…a saddle?"

Hugh's face fell. "Oh."

Beth almost laughed, but knew better than to kick a man when he was down. What sort of a spy was he? He seemed just as capable as getting into scrapes as out of them.

"You had better go speak to that farmer friend of yours," she said, taking another step closer. "I'll stay here with the horse."

"Zeus," corrected Hugh with a sigh. "I knew I'd forgotten something. Won't be long."

He strode off in the direction the farmer had taken, leaving Beth with the horse.

It looked at her. She smiled weakly. "Hello, Zeus."

For a moment, she wondered whether it would charge. It was so much bigger than her, so much stronger. Then slowly, inch by inch, the horse lowered his head until its muzzle gently rested on her shoulder.

Beth gasped, then slowly raised a hand to pet the huge animal. "H-Hello."

By the time Hugh returned with a saddle over his shoulder and a very red face, Beth knew two things. Firstly, Zeus was not going to hurt her. And secondly, she was going to need an impromptu riding lesson, fast.

"Oh, it's easy," said Hugh breezily, adjusting the saddle on the horse's back. "Just like walking, only less injurious to the feet. Ready?"

Beth started. She wasn't expected to get on the horse now, was she? "Ready for what?"

"Up we go!"

Beth almost screamed, but managed to hold in her terror. He simply acted. His strong hands had come around her waist, and all of a sudden, she was up in the air—and then there was solid ground, or something like it, beneath her, but she was seated.

Beth clutched at Zeus's mane, then hurriedly picked up the reins. She was on a horse. On a horse!

"Excellent, we'll make much better time this way," said Hugh briskly.

He placed a boot in the stirrup and launched himself up. Beth clung to the reins as the saddle shifted, but it appeared her companion was quite comfortable riding bareback. She was carefully nestled in the saddle, astride it like a man, and gave a small start as Hugh's hands came around her.

"Right, I'll take those," Hugh said easily, taking the reins. "And off we go!"

And it was remarkably pleasant, Beth had to admit. She could see so much more of the French scenery from up here, no hedgerows to obscure her view. They certainly made better time, the miles slipping away underneath them with very little effort to herself.

Yet it was also heady. Her body was tucked into Hugh's, and sometimes she could feel the steady thump of his heart. At least, she thought she could. Perhaps it was her own. Being so close to him, enclosed within him, should feel wrong, Beth knew. And yet it felt…perfect.

Even better, it made conversation, no matter the topic, feel far more intimate.

A shiver ran up Beth's spine as Hugh said, "See? I told you this would be better!"

"I suppose you did," said Beth with a laugh. "We'll be back in England in no time. What will you do after you have seen your sister? Stay, or come back here?"

She could not pretend it was an innocent question. Though she had been careful not to mention London, it sparked in her heart, the hope he would visit her. And stay. Never leave…

"You know, I haven't given it much thought," said Hugh vaguely, his breath tickling the back of her neck.

Beth shivered. How would she ever go back to her old life? After she had experienced all this, shared it with Hugh, how could she go back to embroidering cushions and practicing the pianoforte?

How could she ever live without him?

"I suppose I knew I would go back, one way or another," Hugh mused behind her. "But it's taken a while, and I'm not sure of the state of things back home. It will be…strange."

Compassion washed over her. She knew what awaited her: an undoubtedly irate yet grateful sister, a brother-in-law who she was still getting to know but appeared pleasant enough, and a brother who would need time to heal.

But it sounded like Hugh had no one other than his sister to return to. Though now she thought about it, Beth thought darkly, she was pleased his father was not there to welcome Hugh home. A man like that did not deserve a son like Hugh.

And an idea flickered in her mind that Beth could not ignore. Though it was rather an intimate question to ask, she couldn't help herself. She had to know.

"I suppose…I suppose your friends will have missed you greatly," she said.

Well, she couldn't just ask outright, could she? She would have to build up to it…

A cold wind rushed past them and Beth shivered. She would have shivered much earlier, however, if she had known what response it would elicit.

Hugh brought his arms more closely around her and the warmth of his body spread through her. Beth breathed in his heady scent and tried to remember what he had told her about staying balanced in a saddle.

It would never do to fall merely because she was intoxicated with Hugh…

"I suppose some missed me," said Hugh quietly. "Though in truth, I have few friends."

This surprised her so much, Beth looked over her shoulder. Her cheeks pinked to find Hugh's face so close to her own. "Few friends? You?"

"I am not always as charming as you have found me," he teased.

But Beth was hardly going to allow that to suffice. As they trotted along the road, no buildings yet in sight, she prompted, "But you…well, you are charming, Hugh."

He grinned.

"You know what I mean!" Beth said, cheeks scarlet. "I just—I would have thought a man like you, with money, with charisma—"

"You forget, I am a—I mean, my family is not well-respected," he said hastily.

There was a hesitation there that she could not ignore. *A what? A spy?*

"Not well-respected?"

"You've heard about my father. You think society could accept such a man?" Hugh's voice was dark, all mischief gone. "In fact, all the men in my family have had a reputation for...well. For lying. Cheating. Ill-gotten gains, and all that. Unwelcome at every door."

Beth's eyes widened. Strange. When they were not facing each other, when she could not look him in the eye, Hugh seemed happier to speak on this delicate topic.

"But you're not like that," she said softly.

Hugh's laugh was just as dark as his voice had been. "You don't know that."

"I know you far better than I know most people, and everything I've discovered, I've liked," Beth admitted.

It was difficult, being this open, this vulnerable. Particularly as she was essentially sitting in his arms. But she couldn't allow him to think this about himself—allow him to believe he was—what had he said? Unwelcome at every door?

"You'd be welcome at my door," she found herself saying.

Hugh barked a laugh. "I'll remind you of that."

"I didn't mean—"

"I know what you meant," he said, his voice softer. "And I thank you, Beth, but it's not been my experience of the world. Being a...coming from my family, with such disgrace in every generation, it's easier not to make friends. They never wish to sully their reputation with mine. It's swifter just to have no friends than to lose them when they realize society will discredit them merely for being in my company."

Beth's heart ached for him as they rode together in silence for a few minutes.

Well, that certainly explained a great deal. For although Hugh was charming, there were certain aspects of how he interacted with the world, she thought, that proved he had spent much time alone. He was lonely.

The affection in her heart began mingling with real concern. Here was a man who had cut himself off from the world merely because he worried about damaging the world's reputation.

"You said once that every spy, every man had his price," she said softly.

Beth felt, as well as heard, Hugh's chuckle.

"Oh, I wouldn't go quoting me," Hugh said. "That's a recipe for disaster."

"I just wondered if…well, if for some people, that price is worthy paying," Beth said hesitantly. Should she be saying this? But it was in her heart, why not speak it? "I mean, losing society's good graces. I mean, I'm hardly in them to start with, so I wouldn't mind —"

"Elizabeth Mead," said Hugh quietly, a tinge of merriment in his voice. "Are you asking me whether I have a lady friend back in England?"

Beth's cheeks burned and her lungs tightened. She was, but she had not expected him to pick up on that so quickly.

Oh, the trouble she ran into with a man just as quick as her!

"N-No, I would never—it would be most inappropriate to even think about ask—"

"Because you can just ask, you know," Hugh said, cutting across her as he guided Zeus along a left hand turn. "I will tell you."

Beth's cheeks burned all the more. What was she doing, playing with this fire?

There was a price for flirting with a gentleman, and if they had been in London, she would be paying it. The whole of society would be gossiping about her inappropriate behavior, and if she wasn't the sister-in-law to a duke, she would receive the Cut.

But this wasn't London. All the norms of society were elsewhere, and she was here, riding a horse with a man's arms around her. A man who had already told her that he liked her. A man who had kissed her. A man who, only yesterday, had said he would do anything for her.

Beth swallowed. "Well, do you?"

"Do what?"

"Hugh Shardlow!"

Her inelegant elbow to his stomach made Hugh's response a little breathless.

"Good God, do you think I would have kissed you if I had another woman stashed about the place in England?"

Beth glanced over her shoulder, hating how glad his answer made her. "Truly?"

Hugh held her gaze. There was no teasing merriment in his expression now. "Truly."

She could have kissed him. Beth was in half a mind to do just that, if not for the fact she was almost certain she would fall off Zeus immediately.

Turning back to the horse's head, she patted the beast. "Right. Well."

"You know, nice young ladies don't typically ask that sort of question."

"But you said—"

"I didn't say you shouldn't, I was just pointing out how different you are from all the dull, yawning ladies who all look the same and speak the same. Those I have had the misfortune in meeting before you," Hugh said quietly.

Beth grinned. "I have always found that acting like a nice young lady is far less fun."

# CHAPTER THIRTEEN

HUGH NARROWED HIS eyes as he looked along the horizon. "Do you see anything?" asked the quiet, weary voice of the woman resting in his arms.

He swallowed. It had been difficult enough to concentrate when she was silent. Never before had he ridden like this, with a woman leaning in his arms, warm and welcoming. There had been moments that day when he had regretted purchasing Zeus.

Not long moments. Most of the time was spent trying not to think about how intimate they were being, how scandalous it would be if they had ridden this way in Hyde Park.

But here, in the middle of nowhere, France?

"Hugh?"

"No, I can't see anywhere that would be suitable," said Hugh hastily, remembering Beth was waiting for an answer.

"Blow," came her gentle reply.

Worry prickled up Hugh's spine. Night was falling fast around them but he had evidently taken a wrong turn somewhere. Though he'd thought his memory of this part of France was relatively good, he had expected a small town by now. Even a village, where a family may have taken pity on Beth and given her shelter for the night.

As it was, a slow drizzle was pouring down his neck, he was

tired, and his bones ached. He couldn't help but presume that Beth was in a similar state. Yet no inn, or any building, could be seen in any direction.

"We'll lose the light soon," said Beth softly.

Hugh nodded. "I know. We'll find somewhere."

He spoke as confidently as he could manage, though he could not see what he was supposed to do about the lack of accommodation.

That was the thing with adventures, a small voice in the back of his mind whispered. They were all well and good in novels, or on the stage. But when living in one, it was astonishing how quickly one became disheartened when unable to find a place to sleep.

"We could always go back—"

"No," said Hugh firmly. Zeus continued to trot along the lane, head lowered. "We've come a long way, but there are still many places we need to look for your brother. Going back would only waste time."

Even if it would bring them to an inn, he thought. It was tempting. Perhaps, when the light completely went…

But what was he thinking? This wasn't London, where gas lamps had been recently fitted and in places the evening air was brilliantly lit, allowing revelers to easily find their way home.

They were in the middle of nowhere. Once they lost the light, they would lose all sense of direction. He was no spy; he could not navigate by the stars, even if Beth assumed he could.

"What's that?"

Hugh's head jerked up. "What?"

"Over there." Beth pointed to something on their right. "I thought I saw…yes, there!"

As Zeus trotted forward, a break in the trees brought a building into view.

And not just a building. Even from this distance, Hugh could see it was an impressive manor, at least three floors high with mock crenellations along the roof. The windows glowed, reflecting the dying sun, and there appeared to be a stable or some outbuildings to the side.

"Hmmm," said Hugh.

It certainly looked striking. If he had been traveling in France under his real name, he would likely as not be able to march up there, reveal himself, and demand entrance. As it was…

"Do you think they would offer us shelter?" asked Beth, tilting her head.

Hugh smiled, his heart lurching as rain dripped off her nose. "Right now, I would say it's worth a try."

He had to admit, in the privacy of his mind, he was not convinced. They were dressed…well, Beth's gown had seen better days, even if it was elegant and stylish. His clothes were French, true, but had attracted much mud over the last few days, and he had a horrible feeling the owners of such a place would not necessarily welcome strangers.

But there were few other options. Within a few minutes, they found themselves trotting up a long gravel drive, the house growing larger and larger.

Beth shifted in the saddle. Hugh did not have to see her face to know her mood. That was the thing with Beth. She rarely hid her emotions, and after their time together—*was it really only a week?*—he could read her like a book.

"You don't have to worry," he said softly.

Beth turned with fear in her eyes. "They'll send us on our way, you know they will."

Hugh cleared his throat. If two such looking miscreants had turned up at his house in the growing dark, he would have sent them on their way. But he couldn't say that.

"We don't have to apply at the house," he said. "We could try an outbuilding—"

"Hugh, look!"

Once again, Beth was pointing, but this time, Hugh did not need any explanation.

Zeus came to a gentle stop outside the front door and Hugh

looked up in wonder.

The place was abandoned. Nothing gave a building that sort of desolate look other than emptiness. A few windows were boarded up and there was a large chain on the front door. Dust could be seen hanging from the curtains, and undisturbed cobwebs covered the stoop.

"Well, it looks like our luck is in," said Beth with a laugh. "Help me, will you?"

Hugh obeyed, though he couldn't see how they could benefit from such a discovery. If the place was abandoned, there was no one within to request shelter. Although he supposed the outbuildings were—

For an instant, after he had dismounted and as he helped Beth, she slid down his body and stood, breathless, in his arms.

Hugh looked at her. Never before had she presented such a tempting offer. Why, he doubted she would resist him if he—

"Now, where shall we break in?" Beth said firmly, stepping back and looking up at the manor.

Hugh knew he had misheard her. There was no possibility she could have said—

"Hugh? I said, where shall we break in?" said Beth, turning to him with surprise that he had not suggested a particular route.

His mouth was dry. "You cannot be serious!"

"No one else is using the place, and we need it," Beth said decidedly. The weather proved her point as the drizzle started to become heavier. "Come on, I don't want to get soaked, and it's not as though we're going to damage the place, are we?"

Still, Hugh hesitated. There was something different between tricking French soldiers to letting English prisoners go and breaking into the manor of a Frenchman who, though French, was probably more like him than he would care to admit.

A marquess, perhaps. Or a duc. Someone of his status.

And then he looked at Beth. At her damp curls starting to stick to her forehead. At the way she was not quite shivering, but evidently attempting not to shiver. At the way her arms had come about her, desperate to keep warm.

Hugh nodded. "Back door. But first, Zeus."

The barn he found was dry and still had hay within it. After wiping and brushing down the horse, ensuring he had access to water, and noting that if they couldn't get into the house, the barn would do just as well, Hugh strode out of the barn and around the house.

"You really think the back door will be unlocked?" said Beth, her teeth chattering.

Hugh tried not to smile. It was the one criticism he had of his servants—and, from the conversation he had shared with other nobles and titled gentlemen in the Dulverton Club, it was a failing of all servants everywhere.

"Most servants don't bother to lock the back door," he said aloud, stepping through a side gate and wandering along a wall covered in wisteria. "They use it as a way to get in and out easily—"

"How on earth would you know that?" asked Beth curiously at his shoulder.

Hugh hesitated. That was an excellent question. "I just know things."

Pathetic an excuse as it was, it appeared Beth was too cold and tired to question him further. "And is it unlocked?"

Stopping before the large oak door with an ornate handle, Hugh took a deep breath and prayed as he reached for the handle. It turned. The door shifted.

"Yes," he breathed with a grin. "Come on in."

It was eerie, stepping into a house that was not your own when you had not been invited. But at least it would mean they could be confident of being undisturbed.

"Goodness," breathed Beth, as though frightened the true owners of the place may startle them at any moment. "And this is just for their servants?"

An odd prickling discomfort spread through Hugh's chest. He had just been about to say how small and pokey the servants' quarters were. He certainly would never have given them such a small, dark, dank place to relax after their hard work.

"I…suppose so," he said awkwardly. "Come on, let's go into the house proper."

"You know, I have never been in a place like this," said Beth in awe, looking around with wide eyes as they stepped along a servants' corridor. "I mean, my brother-in-law's house is large, but I've never been in the servants' quarters. Obviously I've been invited to Lady Romeril's parties"—Hugh's heart skipped a beat—"but Nancy forbade me from exploring."

Hugh suppressed a smile as they stepped through a door and went into the hallway.

He could well imagine Beth being told precisely what she could and could not do at Lady Romeril's—and the irritation she would feel at her curiosity being curtailed.

"It's like they just stepped outside, isn't it?" said Beth in a whisper as she gazed about.

She was right. Though the front door had been coated in cobwebs, it must be merely a sign of the season rather than the duration that the place had been abandoned. It was as though the owners had just stepped out into the night, taking their servants with them.

"Well, I think we can take it that we'll be here for the night," said Hugh softly.

Beth grinned. "Goodness, what luxury! If I had known I'd be sleeping here, I would have come to France sooner."

He chuckled as he moved to return to the kitchen. "Come on. Let's see if any food has been left in the pantry."

There wasn't.

"Oh, damn," he sighed heavily. Then, "My apologies, I meant—"

"I know precisely what you meant," Beth said, peering over his shoulder. "When you meet Matthew, you'll see why I am not offended by a man cursing—and what are you talking about? There's plenty here!"

Hugh blinked. The pantry did not change in any way. "What are you—"

"Now there goes a man who has never been hungry," said Beth with a dry laugh. "Go on, find some plates and cutlery, and I shall bring you enough food to provide a feast!"

Hugh walked back in the kitchen, bemused. Beth could not have seen more than he did. Those shelves were almost bare, with naught but scraps and abandoned food surely inedible.

Though her comment stung, even if she could not have known it. As he dug in drawers looking for forks, Hugh could not deny, even to himself, that she was right. He had never gone hungry. At least, not until he had come to France.

It had been impossible to imagine when living his life as a duke. Food was something provided; it appeared on one's plate, carefully cooked and lovingly styled. Sometimes, the problem was not a dearth of food, but rather a surplus.

*Well, how the mighty have fallen,* he thought ruefully as he looked at the mismatched cutlery he had been able to find now lying on the smooth wooden table.

"Can you light a candle?" came Beth's voice from the pantry.

Hugh's fingers closed on the tinderbox in his pocket. Well, he supposed it would be useful after all. Perhaps it was a good thing he hadn't left it in England.

"Oh, what a fine tinderbox."

Hugh whirled around. "It's not—"

"Where did you find it?" asked Beth as she poked her head around the door.

He swallowed. He had not expected to be questioned about it, and so did not have a lie prepared, which was most unfortunate.

"Looks like it's got a fine crest on it too," she continued with a grin. "You didn't cheat someone out of it at cards, did you?"

Hugh smiled weakly at the excuse offered to him ready made. "Yes. Yes, something like that."

"Here we go!" said Beth cheerfully. "Righty, let's see what we have."

It did not look any more impressive now that it was laid on the table, Hugh could not help but think. It had looked paltry in the pantry, and now looked even smaller on the large expanse of the servants' hall.

"Dig in," said Beth with a grin, pulling at some bread that looked moldy to him.

"We can't eat this," Hugh said softly as he sat on the bench opposite her.

Beth looked up in surprise. "Can't eat—have you never seen three-day old bread before? Or cured meats, dried out to last a while? And this butter has been left in what I think was an ice bucket, it's cold to the touch and perfectly fine. And these apples!"

She lifted one up and displayed it as though it were a huge diamond.

"It's an apple," said Hugh flatly.

Beth grinned. "It's a feast, is what it is!"

And though Hugh had absolutely no reason to believe her, he was rather astonished to find that she was right.

Oh, the bread was a little dryer than he was accustomed to—but when slathered with the butter, which was remarkably fresh, Hugh found he could stomach it quite easily. The meat was delicious, tangy and rich, though he wasn't sure what it was. And though he'd had his doubts, ending his meal with two apples was perfect. Hugh could not recall a dessert he had enjoyed so thoroughly, even when dining with other dukes.

"Well," said Beth quietly. "Was that a meal to remember?"

Hugh's stomach lurched. Not because the food had indeed been bad, but because it had been a meal to remember. Not that it had anything to do with the food itself.

No, it was the company which had breathed such life into the festivities. Their conversation, the way she laughed at his terrible jokes, the lightness she brought to his soul…

Hugh could not recall ever being so at ease.

True, he had rarely dined out, and even more rarely entertained. Few people would accept an invitation from a Martock, after all. Few people extended them.

So he discovered that, over the years, he had grown accustomed to his own miserable company. Dwelling on the past, on the father he had hated and the family line he despised. Thinking of the future had felt a fool's errand, something only those with hope could enjoy.

But now…

"You are thinking of something momentous," said Beth with a grin. "And I demand to know what it is."

Hugh snorted. "Of course you do."

"Well, why wouldn't you tell me?" she asked with a raised eyebrow. "There are so few secrets between us, after all. I'm rather honored a spy would trust me with so much."

And the discomforting feeling in Hugh's stomach reared its head.

He had never lied to her, he told himself firmly. She had guessed, he had denied it—truthfully—and she had chosen to completely ignore everything he had said to the contrary.

It was maddening.

It was a good thing, Hugh thought, Beth would never find out the truth.

"Hugh Shardlow!"

"Fine, fine," he said hastily, lifting his hands in mock surrender, though privately deciding he would not tell her what had actually been going through his mind at that moment. "I was just…I was thinking how proud I am of you."

The words had slipped out, avoiding his better judgment and entirely rushing past his nature before he could stop them. Heat tingled up his chest, but there was nothing he could do now. The words were spoken.

Beth looked self-conscious, her cheeks pinking. "Y-You are?"

"Few sisters would have done half of what you have already achieved in search of your brother," he said earnestly, hating how artless he was being. "You truly are impressive."

Beth looked at her hands for a moment, and suddenly, all the warmth had left the room. He didn't know how, but somehow, Hugh had said something wrong.

"I-I didn't mean to offend—"

"And you didn't," Beth said hastily, looking up with a wry smile. "It's more that…well. I was actually thinking, as we searched for somewhere to stay tonight…that perhaps it would be best if we…if I went home."

It was a good thing Hugh had not been holding any cutlery, for he certainly would have dropped it.

Went home?

This was not the Beth he knew. The Beth he had grown to care for, to feel deep affection for, perhaps even to love? *That* Beth would have dug her heels in and remained in France until every single stone had been turned in search of her brother.

And now she was considering giving up?

It was a jolt to his heart Hugh had not expected. "But you can't!"

"Oh, do not worry, I shall ensure your passage is paid too," said Beth quickly, misunderstanding him. "I am grateful for all the help you have given me, but—"

"You can't give up now; we must be closer than ever before!" Hugh found himself saying, passion pouring into his voice. "Beth, you have to keep going!"

"I'm tired, Hugh."

Hugh swallowed. He could hear the exhaustion in her voice.

This was not the life for a lady. It was hardly the life for a duke. He was accustomed to his own home comforts, and it was wearying for him to go day after day without proper respite, night after night in makeshift beds or lumpy inn mattresses.

But he could also see the pain in her eyes. Beth believed herself to have failed, and he would not allow it.

"You have done incredible things to get here," Hugh said quietly, reaching out his hand to take hers. It was warm. Her fingers quickly entangled with his. "And I am certain, with every bone in my body, that you will find him. And I will be there with you."

Beth's eyes widened. "You...you will?"

Hugh hesitated. These were words he had never intended to say, not to anyone.

But time had changed that, hadn't it? Time with Beth had changed that.

From the moment he had met her, he had been surprised, impressed, and frustrated, almost all at the same time. She never knew when to stop, never thought twice before rushing into a situation, and she cared deeply about the people she loved.

And he wanted to stay by her side. It was where he belonged, somehow. Hugh could not have explained it to anyone, let alone himself.

But until she ordered him away, and perhaps even then, he would not leave her.

"You want to kiss me, don't you?"

Hugh started. Beth was giving him a knowing look, one he was starting to understand well.

He sighed heavily. "Yes. Damnit, Beth, at any given moment of the day and night, I want to kiss you. I think I've made that perfectly clear."

His loins tugged, but he did his best to ignore them. This was not the time to give into that particular urge. Beth was a lady, and—

"And if I wanted you to kiss me?" she breathed, her eyes glittering with mischief but also longing. "What then?"

# CHAPTER FOURTEEN

"*A*ND IF *I wanted you to kiss me? What then?*"

Beth tried to steady her breathing, but it was impossible. It was hard to comprehend how she had spoken so boldly—but then, perhaps those who knew her best would not be surprised. After all, it was not as though she frequently held her tongue or managed to stop herself from speaking her mind.

And Hugh was just...staring at her.

*"And if I wanted you to kiss me? What then?"*

Beth bit her lip. He looked as though he had been struck by lightning. That odd vagueness in his eyes. The way he hadn't blinked since she had spoken. The grip he had on her hand...

Oh, she knew what she wanted. Beth had never been found in a scandalous position with a gentleman, but she knew precisely what ladies of good breeding should not do.

If one wished to stay in society, something Nancy had attempted but rarely managed, ladies were not even supposed to think about being kissed, let alone permit it.

And she had done more than permit it...

"You...you want me to kiss you?" repeated Hugh, his voice hoarse.

Heat tinged Beth's cheeks. Of course, she had been foolish to even think it, let alone suggest it. What had she been thinking? No gentleman of good breeding—and apparently, the Shardlow family was disgraceful, but nonetheless genteel—would accept it.

She should have just kept her mouth shut. Then they could have finished their meal quietly, ventured upstairs to find separate bedchambers, and slept the night away. As it was—

"Did you mean—"

"Forget I said anything," said Beth hastily, rising from the bench and wishing her stomach wasn't twisting so painfully. "It was silly, I shouldn't have—"

"Because it's what I have been hoping you would say," said Hugh, still seated at the table. "For a long time."

Beth bit her lip as she turned back to him.

Did he know what he was saying? Did she understand? There were plenty of opportunities for misunderstandings here, and it simply wouldn't do to get confused…

"No, you don't—I am going to bed," Beth said firmly, cheeks now burning.

Well, she had made a complete fool of herself, and she would have to face him tomorrow in the brightness of day, but that didn't mean she had to face him now. No, she could disappear now, flee the intensity of his gaze.

Beth started toward the door, which she knew led to the corridor to the hall.

And she had almost reached it. Her hand had stretched out for the handle when someone pulled her around.

She gasped. Hugh was standing right before her, eyes blazing with something she did not understand.

Beth tried to take a step back and her ankle tapped the wall just as her back met it. Hugh advanced, and as she moved to take a step to the right, toward the door, toward her escape—he placed his hands on the wall on either side of her.

"Beth," he growled, eyes fixed on her.

Her breath was caught in her throat, her mind whirling, and all she could think about was the intensity of his presence. The way his chest was pressed up against her own. The way she could see nothing in the room except his face.

"Hugh," she breathed.

For some reason, the mere mention of his name was enough to make Hugh groan. He dipped his head for a moment, and in that instant, Beth was certain he was going to kiss her—

Only when he did not did she realize just how much she craved it.

"Beth, I told you before, I like you," Hugh said in a low, dark voice.

"And I said I like you, and—"

"And when I last stole a kiss from you, I told you I wouldn't kiss you again until you gave permission," he continued as Beth's eyes widened. "I think you want more. Don't you?"

Beth hesitated.

Of course she did. More of Hugh? Like she had craved food, as she had desired rest. The same ache flowed through her body, the same need.

And yet it was different. There was a warmth in her chest, a strange patter in her heart, a tingle of anticipation rippling over her skin.

She knew if she did not speak up now, she would regret it. Had she not always wanted an adventure? Was that not one of the reasons, really, that she had come here, to France?

Not just to find her brother. But to find herself.

"I...I want you, yes," Beth said hesitantly, her cheeks aflame but her gaze fixed on Hugh's. "Oh, it seems so shameful to admit—"

"Not shameful at all. Brave, I would call it," Hugh said with a smile.

His hands were still on either side of hers on the wall and Beth shivered to feel so enclosed by him. If it were anyone else, it would be panic filling her lungs, but this was Hugh. She had never felt in danger with him.

Except, of course, that she was in very great danger of falling in love with him.

Beth bit her lip. She was not about to admit that, not to anyone.

"We are alone here," Hugh began.

"We've been alone most of the journey," Beth corrected, lungs tight.

Her hands were placed against the cool of the wall, but the temptation to splay them across his chest was growing. Slowly, very slowly, Beth removed her hands from the wall and did just that.

He groaned. She gasped. His heart was racing, perhaps faster than her own.

What did he want?

Beth pushed aside the thought. She knew precisely what he wanted from her—and she wished to give it. If only there was a way to prevent any…well. Consequences…

"I want to show you just how…how deep my regard is for you," Hugh said quietly. "And I can take precautions."

Beth blinked. "Pre…precautions?"

Hating how her cheeks burned, certain she looked a complete fool, Beth's hands unconsciously gripped Hugh's lapels. Holding onto him somehow made this all feel more real.

"Let me show you how I feel about you," Hugh murmured, his head dipping again. Beth gasped as he kissed her neck. "Let me, Beth. I promise you, you won't regret it."

Beth's eyelashes fluttered as she tried to think past the waves of pleasure now rippling down her neck, sparking her whole body into life.

How could she concentrate when Hugh was doing that? It was tantalizing, the way his hands were not touching her, just pinning her to this part of the wall. Something heady and intoxicating about the way his lips trailed down her neck toward her décolletage.

And the warmth Beth had not understood in her stomach was pooling between her legs, an ache starting to build there, and she knew what she wanted. The question was, was she brave enough to ask for it?

"You said before that every duke, every spy I mean, has his price," Beth said, trying desperately to focus but finding it more difficult with every passing moment. "Is this yours?"

And Hugh lifted his head immediately, his eyes fierce. "Absolutely not—I would never—Beth, you are the one in control here."

She laughed. "I certainly don't feel it!"

Control? She had never felt more out of control in her whole life!

But Hugh's eyes were serious. "You own me here, Beth. I would never—this is nothing to do with our previous agreement. I will help you find your brother no matter how this evening ends. You are the one in charge here, Beth; you can stop me at any moment. Forbid me to touch you, order me away. If you dare."

Beth swallowed. She did not dare. Walking away from Hugh right now would be agony, something she would regret for the rest of her life. No matter what happened, Hugh would never hurt her. He valued her more than that.

"I-In that case," Beth said, fingers trembling as they clung onto Hugh's lapels. "Kiss me, Hugh."

With a growl, he leaned down, nose grazing hers. Just before their lips met, he halted.

Beth whimpered. *Oh, so close…*

"Just kiss you, Beth?" Hugh murmured, his breath warm on her lips, making the ache inside even worse. "Because I want far more. I want to love you, love you as a man loves a woman. All the way."

"All the way."

"Yes, I'm asking—"

"And I'm answering," said Beth, hardly knowing how she was being this bold, but knowing she was speaking the truth. "I want you, Hugh. All of you."

No more words were possible, and she was relieved, for Hugh had pressed his lips against hers, and it was sweet relief after the tension between them. Tension Beth had hardly known was there, but now that it was over, she wondered how they had managed to pass a single minute together without giving into the temptation.

Because she loved him. Beth didn't know when it had happened. Perhaps when he had first kissed her, perhaps when he had rescued that cat, then shared his story. Perhaps when he had protected her, cared for her, made her laugh.

Perhaps it was all the times put together.

All she knew was that as she stood here, pinned between the wall and Hugh's chest pressed up against hers, Beth knew she was precisely where she belonged.

"Beth," Hugh moaned.

His hands left the wall, one cupping her face, the other resting on her waist. Beth's hands somehow managed to get tangled in his hair, fingers trailing down his nape, pulling him desperately closer.

Warmth was spreading through her, red-hot heat. Beth wanted more, and she kissed him eagerly, her lips parting as she welcomed him in.

"Oh God, I've wanted this so long," Hugh muttered, releasing her lips only to kiss just below her ear.

Beth chuckled as she held him, head tilted back, overcome with pleasure. "How can you, we only met a few weeks ago?"

"And the instant I saw you, I wanted you," muttered Hugh. "And each day I've grown to know you better, that need has only increased. Damn, Beth..."

How long they stood there kissing against the wall, Beth did not know. Time had ceased to have any meaning. Not when she was in Hugh's arms.

But eventually, he broke their kiss and pressed his forehead against hers. "Christ, Beth. I never know I could feel such—"

"I know," she breathed. "I feel it too."

They were both panting. Beth wondered if the same exhilaration filling her bones was rushing through him. Was this what it was to be loved? To be craved, so desired that the whole world seemed to be designed for their pleasure?

Glittering wickedness sparkled in Hugh's eyes. "I could take you against the wall—"

"Hugh!"

"—but I think I would rather have something a little softer for your first time," he continued with a mischievous chuckle. "Come on. Let's see what bedchambers they have."

He took her hand in his own, so naturally Beth wondered why he hadn't before.

And then Hugh was pulling her through the door into the corridor, along the corridor, into the hallway, and up the stairs.

Beth's heart thundered in her chest, her breathing short, but it was excitement and not panic that held sway over her throbbing body. Excitement for what they had already shared, and excitement for what was to come.

The upstairs of the manor they had broken into was cavernous in the dark gloom of the evening. Beth looked around. Every door looked the same.

"Let's try this one," Hugh said, striding forward and pulling her along with him.

The door looked just the same as all the others from what Beth could see, but somehow, Hugh seemed to know his way about this manor. Perhaps all manors were the same, she thought wildly, though that did not explain—

"As I thought," Hugh said, pulling her through the door. "The main bedchamber."

And Beth gasped.

It certainly was. At least, she could not imagine another bedchamber more impressive than this.

A huge four-poster bed was against the wall. Its hangings appeared, in the low light, to be dark blue velvet. The coverlet on the bed was still there, left as though its owner would return in a matter of moments.

If they did, they would behold a magnificent room. All the

furniture appeared to be gilt gold, there were beautiful landscapes hanging on the walls, and the wallpaper itself appeared to be painted gold and leather. There were elegant ornaments on every surface, a resplendent chaise longue—

"Stop looking at your surroundings," came Hugh's voice with a growl. "And kiss me."

Beth happily obliged. It felt bold to be reaching up her lips and kissing a gentleman, but Hugh was no gentleman. In this moment, he was just a man, and she was just a woman. Two people who desired each other, who could no longer resist.

Desire billowed in Beth's chest, and as she kissed Hugh, her tongue met his and she shivered at the intensity. This was what she wanted. All she wanted.

Her hands moved down his chest, carefully unbuttoning—

"Dear God, Beth," Hugh moaned.

Beth immediately halted. Cheeks burning, she stepped back. "I-I am sorry, I didn't mean to—"

"Do you have any idea how erotic it is, finding a woman who wants me as much as I want her?" Hugh said, his hair mussed and his eyes dancing with desire. "Dear God, it's more than I could ever have dreamed!"

Beth smiled, nerves immediately transforming into relief as she stepped back to him, continuing to unbutton his waistcoat.

She had always presumed a woman's desire was…unseemly. Unwanted. Unnecessary, at least from the very basic instructions her mother, pink in the face throughout their whole conversation, had given.

But this was different. Here, they were equals. Two people who both wanted pleasure, and Beth now knew she would not be chastised for showing it.

Both Hugh's coat and waistcoat were swiftly dropped to the floor. Only then did Beth realize that while she had been busy disentangling irritatingly complicated buttons—something about kissing made it very hard to concentrate—Hugh had been equally busy.

Her gown slipped from her shoulders.

"Hugh!" Beth gasped, but it was too late.

The ribbons and ties at the back of her gown were entirely undone, and so was she. Her gown fell to the floor, swathes of silk and lace, and there she stood in her undershift, corset, and stays.

She had expected, when or if she ever found herself in such a situation, to feel embarrassed. But as Beth met Hugh's eye, she felt nothing but…desired. It was impossible to feel anything else when a man like Hugh was looking at her like that.

"Oh, Beth, you're so beautiful," he moaned.

Beth smiled nervously. "In that case, you'll like this even more."

How her fingers managed to remove her undershift, leaving her in just corset and stays, she had no idea—but the effort was well worth it.

Hugh's eyes fluttered shut for a moment as he pulled off his boots and started scrabbling at the buttons of his breeches. "Go and lie on the bed, Beth—before I put you there."

Though a thrill rushed through her at the idea of being put there by Hugh, Beth stepped over to the bed.

It really was huge. Heart in her mouth, warmth growing between her legs, Beth clambered onto the bed and lay on her back, hearing the rustle of fabric.

Then she gasped.

"Beth," Hugh breathed, climbing onto the bed with her.

He was utterly naked. Beth's eyes were dragged to the one part of a man she knew she absolutely should not be looking at, but if not now, when would she ever get the chance?

His manhood stood ready for her, enclosed in something.

"Wh-What is—"

"It's called a French letter," said Hugh, his voice rasping as he pulled her into him, their legs tangling together. "It'll prevent any…consequences."

Beth nodded, hands pressed against his chest. Oh, this was

glorious—there was surely nothing more intimate than this! Lying on a bed together, Hugh completely naked, her only with her undergarments on. Surely nothing could—

"Let's free you from that, shall we?" said Hugh in a low voice.

Beth gasped as his fingers made short work of her corset. It burst open, revealing her breasts, which immediately transfixed him.

"Oh, Beth…"

Beth whimpered, her back arching as Hugh lowered his mouth to one of her breasts, his lips capturing her nipple.

Pleasure, pleasure such as she had never known, was roaring through her. Instincts were taking over. Hugh was somehow nestled between her legs, his elbows keeping him raised as his mouth moved to her other breast.

"Oh, Hugh, yes," Beth moaned, unable to hold it in.

And what did it matter? No one could hear them. She could be as loud as she liked.

"Hugh, God, yes—"

Hugh lifted his head. "Beth, I can't—are you ready for me—you definitely want—"

"Get inside me, now," Beth breathed, hardly knowing where these words came from.

A deep, dark place within her had opened and she wanted nothing more now than to be one with the man giving her such sweet delights.

Swiftly, Hugh kissed her hard on the lips. "You complete me, Beth. Before I even enter you, I can tell you that—you are everything, you—oh, Beth!"

Beth cried out too, though her voice was more guttural as Hugh's manhood pressed into the soft warm wet between her legs.

And though she had expected pain, there was nothing.

Well, not *nothing*. Sparks of unexpected pleasure, rippling sensual decadence, were flowing through her body as he slowly slipped into her.

Beth clutched at the bedsheets, hardly knowing what was to come next. There could not be any greater pleasure, could there? This was surely the pinnacle!

Hugh was breathing hard, fully sheathed inside her. "Damn. Oh, Beth—"

"Kiss me," she demanded, astonished at her own bluntness but knowing he would not be dismayed.

Quite to the contrary, it appeared Hugh was driven even more mad by her demand. He kissed her hard on the mouth and she almost cried out as he started to withdraw himself—

"Hugh!"

He had plunged back into her, and a glimpse of ecstasy passed through her.

Beth blinked, hardly able to take it in. Hugh was grinning.

"Ready?" he growled.

"Are you?" she shot back.

Hugh dipped his mouth to hers as his manhood slid almost completely out of her and then plunged into her again. And again. And again.

Beth could do nothing but cling onto his shoulders as he started to build a rhythm that soared her onto the edge of something splendid. God, this was wonderful—every movement of his manhood teased her, promised something greater then drew away from it, and as her body started to tingle all over and the pleasure almost overwhelmed her—

"Hugh, Hugh, oh God, yes!"

And Beth exploded.

At least, that was what she assumed had happened. Every part of her catapulted over the crest of ecstasy Hugh had been promising her with his body, and he jerked and poured himself into her as she clung to him, hardly able to think as her body pulsed with pleasure.

And it was over. Hugh fell into her arms, and Beth held him, knowing that what they had shared was something she would never forget.

The love of a good man. Who could put a price on that?

# CHAPTER FIFTEEN

*October 10, 1810*

"AND YOU ARE sure about this?" asked Hugh, just a little hesitancy in his voice. "You don't have to—"

"I'm sure," said Beth, her voice heavy but head held aloft. "It's time to go home."

The lane they were trotting along on Zeus was narrow and winding, giving them little opportunity to see what was ahead. Hugh was attempting to concentrate on the road, ensure they were unlikely to run into a cart, a carriage, people walking along the side of the path.

But that was difficult, considering the conversation they were having.

Hugh swallowed. It was hard to believe it was only days since they had shared the most intimate moments he could imagine.

*"You complete me, Beth. Before I even enter you, I can tell you that—you are everything, you—oh, Beth!"*

He had not quite believed Beth understood what she was willing to give up when she had opened herself for him and permitted him to—

*"Dear God, it's more than I could ever have dreamed!"*

A flicker of remembered pleasure roared through him,

though it faded in the light of day as though it had not been there.

What they had shared…it was something Hugh would never forget. A closeness, a moment of true clarity he had never expected.

He wanted to be with this woman. With Beth. Not just today, or tomorrow, but for the rest of his life. The thought of the future without her was so abhorrent, Hugh wondered how he could ever have considered it.

And now, with Beth sitting once more in his arms as they rode Zeus together, it was almost impossible to believe that this very morning, she had made the decision she had.

But he was not dreaming.

"We make for the sea," Beth said, her voice unwavering. "And find a ferry."

Hugh wished they were facing each other, wished he could see her expression. It had been a surprise to him when she announced she was giving up her search for her brother.

"Time to go back home," she had said quietly. "Time to accept one woman cannot search the entirety of France and—"

"But you were always so determined," Hugh had blurted out. "So eager to find him, so sure—"

"Well, I am not sure anymore," Beth had said, a faint smile on her lips. "And if I have one of the most impressive men I have ever met alongside me, and I still cannot find him…perhaps Matthew cannot be found. Perhaps he does not want to be found."

Hugh had hated the despair in her voice.

No, not quite despair. It was worse than that. Resignation.

That had been then. A few hours of riding toward the coast had followed that conversation. Hugh was not entirely sure whether Beth was certain about her decision.

He cleared his throat. "Beth, I will keep looking for him with you for as long as—"

"What about our agreement?" came her reply. It was tinged with a little merriment.

It was the merriment that twisted Hugh's stomach. Strange, how swiftly the roles could be reversed. Ever since he had made her acquaintance, he had been—harshly, perhaps—trying to make Beth realize her brother may not be discoverable. That she may have to return to London, at some point, without him.

And she had argued with him, had she not? Been determined, absolutely, to find him.

Now they appeared to have taken the other's argument.

"Our agreement was to search for a month, yes," Hugh conceded aloud. "But—"

"Your sister will not wait, her child will arrive whether we find Matthew or not," said Beth with a dry laugh. "You may know a great deal about pleasing a woman, Hugh"—and his cheeks burned—"but you seem to have forgotten some basic biology. You'll be an uncle before too long. Your family needs you."

Hugh opened his mouth, hating that no words came to mind, then closed it again.

*Well, hell.* He had never thought his lie about a sister in confinement would last this long. That was the trouble with being a Martock. Most of the time, the lie you told ceased all connection with the person you were speaking to, and you never saw them again.

So it didn't matter that you had lied.

But with Beth…well, he had half expected her to give up this fruitless hunt within a day or two. Lying about a sister in confinement would have lasted the day to reach the sea, the day of the crossing, and then that would be it. He could melt back into the chaos of London, and she would never need to know he had been untruthful.

As it was…

"Ah. Yes. My sister," he said, hating himself. "Well, if you are determined—"

"I would have thought you would know me better than that by now," said Beth, tilting her head to meet his eye. "Once I have made my decision, I have made it."

A smile quirked Hugh's lips. "I did hear something about that, yes."

"Then we'll keep onward to the sea," she said, turning away. "It is the right decision. I am sure of it."

Hugh tried to hear any hint of concern or regret in her tone, but he heard none.

Or perhaps he just did not know her sufficiently well. It was hard to remember, after all, that he had only met the vibrant, reckless woman a few weeks ago.

"How far, do you think?"

And yet he knew her so well. How she ate food when famished, Hugh thought with a genial smile. How she mistrusted people far longer than they believed. How she rode a horse. How she wanted to be kissed—

"Hugh?"

And that was the trouble, wasn't it? Hugh was starting to discover that though he knew so much about Beth, it wasn't enough. He wanted to know everything. All that made her Beth—

"Hugh, can you hear me?"

Hugh started and Zeus sparked under him, unhappy with the sudden movement.

"He's sorry, Zeus, he was just lost in his thoughts," said Beth, leaning forward to pat the horse's neck. "What were you thinking, Hugh?"

Certainly not something he could tell her. "England. Life there after all this time."

It was not going to be pleasant, Hugh was certain. Oh, the old house would be there. There was enough money in the Martock coffers to keep a place like that running until the end of the world.

No, it was the dull social scene he would have to make an appearance in that he dreaded. Lady Romeril would demand invitations, and he would have to host a dinner.

Hugh tried not to groan. And the dullest people would come, just to have a look at the Duke of Martock. Where had he been? They would all ask. What terrible deeds had he committed?

"England," said Beth with a sigh. "I suppose my sister will be furious."

"Probably, if she is anything like you," Hugh teased.

She turned immediately to glare, only laughing when she saw the mischief in his face. "Hugh Shardlow, I do believe you are ribbing me!"

"I certainly am," said Hugh cheerfully. The sun was starting to come out, and he could see the sea in the distance. It was going to be a wonderful day. "But only a little."

Because he knew, didn't he, that the other Miss Mead, whoever she was, was unlikely to be truly upset with her sister. Not when Hugh revealed himself as a duke and proposed marriage to Beth.

He had to ask her. He couldn't imagine his life without her. Was that not the very purpose of matrimony?

Oh, the *ton* would argue it was about money, prestige, alliances, power. They would expect him to choose a duchess from a noble family who brought plenty of money, perhaps even her own jewels.

But what did he care? Hugh grinned, happiness welling in him. The Duke of Martock never did what anyone in society expected anyway, so why not live up to those wild expectations?

Why not bring home a penniless, brash bride?

"Your sister will be happy to see you, I suppose?"

Hugh barked a laugh. "There will be few in London happy to see me, Beth. I told you before, my father hardly had a pleasant reputation, and all the men in my family…generations of liars and cheats."

He had been too open. Immediately trying to think of a way to ameliorate what he had just said, Hugh tried desperately to think. *Damnit!*

"But you're not like that," said Beth conversationally as Zeus trotted along the road.

There was salt in the air now. Hugh could scent it as he breathed in. They were almost there. The crossing would not take long, and they would be in England. And he could tell her, reveal to the woman he loved—for he did love her, Hugh knew that now—that he was a duke, and that all her problems were over.

Excitement rushed through him. How delighted she would be! How glad he had kept that particular part of him private until he could be sure she held affection for him unsullied by the temptation of a title.

*Or poisoned by the recognition of your title,* Hugh thought. If she knew he was a Martock…

"You seem remarkably happy," commented Beth as they reached the outskirts of the little town nestled against the sea.

Ships were visible in the distance, their rigging flapping and snapping in the wind. Hugh's heart skipped a beat. *Not long now.*

"I do?"

Beth nodded, twisting in his arms to meet his gaze. "Yes. Very happy."

Hugh's stomach tied itself in a knot. "That…that's because I have you."

Why was it so difficult to tell the full truth of the matter? Having Beth in his arms, in his confidence, hopefully before too long in his bed…it was everything he wanted. How strange to think he had come to France merely because he was bored. He had certainly found the remedy to his boredom. He didn't think he would ever be bored again married to Beth.

She beamed at his words. "Truly?"

Hugh responded the only way he knew how. He leaned forward and kissed her hard on the mouth.

Beth clung to him, her balance almost lost as the horse continued along.

Oh, that kiss. It was a kiss of equals, something Hugh had never shared before. He was more noble than her, but only by birth. Beth was the one who was truly noble, whose instincts had never led her wrong as she attempted to do what was right for her brother.

*Well,* muttered a dark voice at the back of Hugh's mind. *She was wrong, except with you.*

Hugh broke off the kiss. "Come on, we should dismount. It'll be easier to get to the docks that way."

Beth's cheeks were bright red as she obeyed, slipping into his arms then stepping out of them, her gaze darting about her.

It was all he could do not to smile. He had hardly noticed anyone else around them, his attention was completely focused on her—but now that he came to think about it, they were in the middle of a busy street. A few curious glances were being shot at them.

Hugh's chest swelled. Let them look. He was kissing the woman he loved, the woman who would soon be his wife. What did he have to hide?

"Careful, Hugh," said Beth quietly.

He glanced over to where she was looking and pulled Zeus toward him, out of the way of the regiment of English soldiers that were marching down the street.

How tired they looked with their red uniforms and dull swords. They had seen battle. Seen the enemy, and probably lost friends, too. Thank the lord he had never—

"Why—it's the Duke of Martock!"

Hugh froze. *Dear God, no.*

"Yes, I thought it was, the Duke of Martock himself! Goodness gracious, what's that old cad doing here?" called out one of the officers.

Hugh's heart had entirely frozen in his chest. It couldn't be. What were the chances someone would recognize him—and now, after almost seven months in the blasted country?

Now, when Beth was by his side?

"What is that man talking about, I wonder," said Beth idly, watching the men pass by.

The officer who had shouted out his name, Hugh saw with a sinking heart, had left the order of the march and was pushing his way through his men. Toward them.

*Toward me,* Hugh thought with a nauseous feeling.

He had to leave—had to get Beth away from here before she heard something he could not explain.

But there was nowhere to go. The marching regiment had pushed all the French townspeople to the sides of the street; they were pinned in—and with Zeus beside them, there was nowhere they could go. What was he going to—

"It almost looks like he's making for us," Beth commented, a hint of curiosity in her voice. "How strange. Perhaps he has mistaken you for—"

"Get back onto Zeus, Beth, we need to go."

She blinked up into his face, astonished at his words. "Go? But—"

"Please, Beth, I am asking this as a favor," Hugh said hurriedly, his words spilling over each other in his haste.

He had to get her out of here; he had to ensure she didn't hear—

"Martock! Goodness, I thought you were in London!" cried the officer, slapping Hugh on the back. "Thought you'd finally come to see what all the fuss was about, eh?"

It was the nightmare Hugh never thought he would have to face. It was the loss of everything he had built, albeit in a small time, with Beth. And it was all going to be destroyed before his eyes.

"Martock?" Beth said, looking between the two men. "I don't know a Martock—who are you, sir?"

Even in the midst of his panic, Hugh had to smile. Trust Beth to speak to an officer like that, all brashness and no deference.

The officer bristled. "I will have you know, young lady, I am Captain Lister of—"

"How very pleasant for you," Beth said, cutting across him with that icy coldness Hugh knew all too well. "On your way."

Hugh's breath caught in his chest. Was it possible—was his luck going to hold? Would Beth never find out the truth merely because she did not like the way the officer spoke to her?

"I merely thought I would speak to His Grace for a moment, I am sure," snapped Captain Lister haughtily. "We are acquainted, after all, even if His Grace will not own me. Lady Romeril introduced us, and—"

"I have no idea what you are talking about," said Beth slowly.

"Beth," Hugh said quietly. "I—"

"There is no duke here, and I think I would know about it if there was!" she continued with a wry smile at Hugh, as though they were both sharing the joke. "Isn't that right, Hugh?"

Hugh tried to smile. That was all he had to do, smile. Make it clear he understood the joke, then Captain Lister could be on his way, and everything would be as it was.

Yet, he could not do it. "Beth—"

"You mean to tell me you don't know this man is the Duke of Martock?" Captain Lister said, astonishment dripping from every word.

Hugh could hardly hear anything save for the words of the two people before him. Panic was rising in his chest, a painful urge to run combatted by the agony of his legs as shame overcame him.

It was all over.

"A duke?" Beth breathed, looking between the two men. "Hugh, what is he—"

"A cowardly duke, to boot," Captain Lister sneered. "The man wouldn't fight for his country! Last I heard, he had come to France to drink wine and find women to—"

"But Hugh is a—he spied for his country, put his life in danger," Beth said hurriedly.

Hugh wished he could stop her, wished he could stop this whole moment, pause time, giving himself a chance to think.

But he couldn't, and the conversation rattled on without him, his chest heaving, his heart thundering painfully.

"A spy?" The captain snorted. "Dear God, no! On a jolly, aren't you, Your Grace?"

"That will be all, Captain, now return to your regiment," Hugh muttered through clenched teeth.

There was a gleam in the man's face, however, that told him in no uncertain terms Captain Lister was well aware of the damage done…and was pleased.

Hell, what had he done to deserve this? Had he accidentally snubbed the man in public? Had he perhaps not joined a card party when he ought, or stepped across the street at just the inopportune time?

Or was this somehow a punishment for all he had ever done? The lies he had allowed Beth to believe, Hugh thought with a sinking feeling. Well, he deserved it.

"Well, I shall be on my way, I'm sure," said Captain Lister icily. "My lady."

And with a curt bow of the head, he was gone.

Hugh's heart appeared to have stopped beating. He was looking at Beth, who was staring with horror.

That was it then. It was all over.

"Hugh," Beth murmured as the sound of marching soldiers disappeared, the regiment gone. "What was that man talking about?"

Hugh swallowed. Why hadn't he just told the truth when she had first asked? No lies about sisters in confinement, no permitting her to believe the falsehood of him being a spy.

It hurt, after all these years, to have his father proven right. He was useless, he was a liar, and he was a cheat. It had just never pained him like it did now, with Beth's disbelief and pain etched across her beautiful face.

"Is it…it's true, isn't it?" she said dully.

It wasn't a question. Hugh had half hoped that she would wish to hear his side of the story. Hear how he had lied once, yes, about the sister. And fine, perhaps by omission by not including his true name.

But it had been she who believed him a spy, even after he had denied it several—

Hugh's shoulders slumped. Oh, what was he trying to prove? Was he truly trying to place the blame for this on her?

Beth had done nothing to deserve this. Worse, she was everything he was not: honest, pure, and good. And he had ruined that. He had caused her to trust, and now the truth of the matter, that she should never have trusted him, was pouring out.

The temptation to lie rose in his heart, but Hugh pushed it aside. He may have proven his awful father right, but that stopped now. He didn't have to be like all the other Martocks who had gone before. He didn't have to stoop to the lowest level.

He had to be honest.

"I am the Duke of Martock," Hugh said quietly. "And as I said to you before, I…I am not a spy."

Beth's eyes were filling with tears, and all he wanted to do was hold her and kiss them away, but that chance had gone. He had destroyed it.

"You…you're not a spy?" she whispered. "You haven't served the country, you aren't—"

"I never told you I was a spy! I'm here because I tired of London life and wanted a distraction," Hugh said wretchedly, hating every word he was saying. "I wanted to be entertained."

And Beth gave a bitter laugh. "And was I? Entertaining enough for you, a sufficient distraction?"

# CHAPTER SIXTEEN

"Y*OU...YOU'RE NOT A spy? You haven't served the country, you aren't—*"

"*I never told you I was a spy! I'm here because I tired of London life and wanted a distraction. I wanted to be entertained.*"

"*And was I? Entertaining enough for you, a sufficient distraction?*"

Beth stared up at the man she had trusted. She'd allowed him to know so much of herself. She had allowed him to...

Her cheeks burned as the memories of that night returned. Memories she thought she would treasure. Memories impossible to sully, for who would have believed Hugh was anything but perfect?

"*You complete me, Beth. Before I even enter you, I can tell you that—you are everything, you—oh, Beth!*"

Yet here she was. Standing in a French town, a horse behind her making it impossible to run away, looking at a man who had lied about...about everything.

"It wasn't like that," said Hugh hastily. "It—"

"I don't want to hear it," Beth said.

Her voice was dull, nothing like the agony within her heart as disappointment seared through her chest. How had she been so foolish?

This was why Nancy had not wished for her to come on her own. Not because she wouldn't find their brother, although that turned out to be true. Not because she couldn't navigate France. Her French was better than her sister's.

No, it was because she, Beth, was too trusting.

*"Ah, there you are. I've been looking for you everywhere."*

Why had she immediately believed a man she met in a French inn? How had she left behind all her sense, ignoring her instincts to do this on her own? Why had she not asked more questions, forced the man to…

But then, she had asked, hadn't she? It all seemed so obvious now.

Why would a man be in such a rush to return for his sister's confinement? A sister, moreover, who he never named. Never spoke of. Hugh never talked about how excited he was to see her, how he felt about becoming an uncle.

All the normal things that a person would say.

And he let her believe so many lies.

"Beth," Hugh said firmly. "You have to believe me—"

"Believe you? Why should I believe you? You've given me no reason to," Beth said sharply, bitter anger rising in her chest. "I don't even know you!"

And the fact which had escaped her notice, which had gotten lost in the sea of betrayal she found herself swimming in, rose to the surface.

*Martock. The Duke of Martock.*

After all this time together, sharing so much of herself, her family, her desires…he hadn't even told her his true name?

"You are the Duke of Martock," Beth said.

It didn't seem possible…yet there had been signs, if she had not been so foolish as to ignore them. The tinderbox she spotted in the manor, it had a crest on it. Why hadn't she bothered to look at it more closely?

But it was more than that. The man hardly knew what money was, meandering around the country with little purpose and even less of a plan. He did not seem to understand, did he, what it was like for her and her family? To struggle, to strive.

The man had probably never worked a day in his life, Beth thought dully. While Nancy had been forced to work. And here Hugh stood, if that was even his name, not appreciating anything he had!

"I am Hugh Shardlow, Duke of Martock."

"Well, I suppose it's a small comfort that you told me half the truth," she couldn't help but say with viciousness.

Beth turned away, no longer able to look at him. Her feet moved forward—she had to get away from him. The docks. Yes, she wanted to leave, now.

"Beth!"

"You, man, will you buy a horse?" Beth said to the nearest Frenchman.

She ignored Hugh's words. How easy it was, after considering herself in love with him, to tune him out. Did that mean she had never loved him? Did that mean her love was so whimsical it could so swiftly disappear?

"A horse?" blinked the Frenchman.

Beth tried to smile, though she had never felt less like smiling in all her life. "I am leaving France and cannot take him with me. Zeus could be yours for—"

"Beth, we need to talk about this—"

"We don't need to talk about anything," she hissed, glaring at Hugh. "There is nothing I want to hear from you. Well?" she added, looking at the Frenchman.

The transaction was complete within a minute.

Beth tried to breathe calmly, but it was impossible. "Th-The docks, monsieur?"

She strode forward in the direction the bemused man pointed, but found she could only make it a few steps before she halted.

There was a hand holding onto her arm.

"Beth, you've got to listen to me," said Hugh hurriedly.

Beth wrenched her arm from his grip. "I don't have to do anything!" she shot back.

She tried not to see the pain in his eyes. *It's all his doing*, she told herself as she marched forward along the street, seagulls squawking in the air. Hugh had the chance to tell the truth, not once, but every day they had been together. It was not her fault he had taken no opportunities. That he had permitted her to believe such lies...

*"You are a spy, aren't you?"*

Beth pushed the memory aside. Yes, well, she had guessed incorrectly—but he had hardly put up much of a fight.

"Well then, you'll just have to listen," said Hugh, doggedly matching her steps as she marched to the docks. "I admit, I lied about my sister. Actually, I lied about having a sister—"

Beth snorted. "Of course you did!"

How had she been so blind? So naïve?

It was a relief in a way that Nancy had not accompanied her. Not that she would have minded, but to have the proof of her stupidity so obvious...no, it was best no one ever learned quite how foolish she had been.

Not only to hand over the responsibility of looking for her brother, but her heart.

"I just didn't want to admit the truth—"

"Of course you didn't, what man would want to admit he had come to France not to fight for his country, but to gad about with women?" Beth stormed, heart breaking as she spoke.

That was all she was to him, wasn't she? A distraction. Entertainment. Something to do to pass the time. Oh, that she had allowed herself to be so easily taken in...

"The truth was, I saw something in you—"

Beth laughed darkly as she turned a corner and saw the docks ahead. A ship, that was what she needed. A ship, to get out of here. She had to leave all this pain and anguish behind.

"You saw a woman with money who could give you what you wanted," Beth said, marching forward. "You, sir, you sail for England?"

"Beth—"

"I am having a conversation with this captain, and you are interrupting," said Beth icily, turning from Hugh and back at the Frenchman. "Well? Do you sail for England?"

"In...in ten minutes, yes—"

"Excellent," said Beth, trying to take a deep breath and hating the way her lungs fought against it. "In that case, Your Grace, you have ten minutes to make your apologies."

Hugh blinked. He appeared completely stunned by her words.

Of course he did, Beth thought as seagulls swooped and the sea rushed against the dock. He had never expected to have to apologize.

"I...well, I—"

"Nine minutes," said Beth sharply.

And a flicker of power, of pleasure at the thought of finally being back in control, washed over her.

Beth swallowed. It was strange, this anger, this bitterness. She was the one who had been betrayed, yet she somehow felt responsible. As though she had not been paying close enough attention. As though if she had just thought about it for five minutes, she would have noticed clues as to Hugh's true identity.

Yet, she hadn't. She had been completely taken in.

Hugh took a deep breath. "Yes, I came to France to distract myself—but you cannot know what it was like, living in London. No one wished to know me, I was excluded from—"

"You mean to tell me that the rich, noble duke was bored of having a poor reputation? So instead of working to improve it, you ran away."

Where this harshness was coming from, she could not tell. Perhaps it was from the broken well of her heart. The ache within her seemed to pour forward like bile.

Hugh flinched. "You make it sound awful."

"Can you not see that, from my perspective, it is?" Beth shot back, heart thundering. "For goodness sake, Hugh, you know my family is not well off! I have been open with you about our struggles, and you—"

"You think money the only thing worth having?" Hugh said, interrupting as his cheeks pinked. "You cannot know what it is to live without affection; you've had it all your life!"

But Beth would not permit him to get away with that. Yes, she'd had two loving parents, and still, God willing, had two loving siblings. But that did not mean she'd had an easy life, and it certainly didn't excuse the lies he had told.

"What, because my parents loved me and yours did not, you can do no wrong?"

"That is not what I—"

"I trusted you, Hugh." Beth hated how her voice broke, but she could not keep it level. He flinched. "I trusted you as a man, a gentleman, a friend, perhaps—well, I thought—"

"You thought?" he said eagerly.

Beth forced aside the emotions that had sprung up in that moment. She had been about to say she had hoped there might be more. That when they returned to England, their acquaintance would not come to an end. That perhaps, it would not remain an acquaintance…

But how could she countenance that now? How could she look at Hugh without feeling betrayed?

Beth caught his gaze, and pain, as sharp as a knife wound, slipped into her chest.

No, she could never trust him now.

"I thought you were a spy," she said quietly as people behind him started to board the ship to England. "I admired you, believed you to be—"

"I told you from the start I had never been a spy, and you would not heed my words," said Hugh, pointing a finger.

Beth stared at it coldly until Hugh's cheeks darkened and he allowed his hand to drop to his side. "Perhaps I did not. But you lied about everything else, didn't you? You don't have a sister, you weren't in England for any noble purpose—"

"I tried to tell you—"

"And you allowed me t-to give you myself," Beth breathed, hardly able to speak above a whisper. "You allowed me to lose my innocence when you knew I didn't even know you."

Hugh took a step back. He looked, for a moment, genuinely aggrieved. For a moment, Beth was glad. She wanted him to feel the weight of his treachery. She wanted him to know just what it was to feel all of one's trust broken.

"It wasn't like that," he murmured, his gaze dropping.

Beth bit her lip. "I don't know what it was," she confessed with a heavy sigh. "I don't know if I can trust anything you said, anything we shared."

"But I—"

"No, Hugh," Beth said, and her voice was suddenly gentle. All the anger, all the bitterness, it had seeped away. All that was left was fatigue. "It's over. Whatever it was we had, whatever you thought it could be…it's gone."

A sea breeze tugged her curls. Beth knew she probably looked an awful state. She would have to hope passage across to England would not deplete her funds to such an extent that she could not afford a carriage back to London.

The rest of her life stretched out before her. Empty.

At least, empty of Hugh. Somehow, even though she still burned with pain at his betrayal, she could have wept for the lack of him. What was her life to be now, without him?

"You're a duke," Beth found herself saying.

Despite all the perhaps more important revelations that the surprising conversation with Captain Lister had brought, this was the one that shone out to her. *A duke.*

Yes, Nancy had married a duke only weeks ago, but that was different. Byron was soft, gentle. Quick to defend, quick to protect.

Hugh? Hugh was bold, and brave. She had thought him the absolute pinnacle of a man, and had allowed him to bruise her heart, and she…

Beth bit her lip again. She would never be the same again.

Hugh had stepped forward, closing the gap between them. Beth longed to be in his arms again. Just one more kiss; it wouldn't matter, would it? Oh, how she craved him. How was it possible to need a man after only knowing him a month?

"Beth, I never meant to lie, or permit you to believe untruths," Hugh said quietly. "I've hardly had the best role models in life—"

"You are a grown man," Beth shot back.

"I'm just trying to be honest here!" Hugh said, his voice breaking. "Being honest, being vulnerable, it's not something I do well, I know, but I am trying!"

Beth swallowed. *Well, that was true, right enough.*

"I thought if you knew the real reason why I had come to France in the first place, you would not wish to know me. That I would lose all chance to get to know you, for you to get to know me, the real me," Hugh persisted.

Beth tried not to look into his handsome face. She didn't want her resolve to be tested, could not fall back into his embraces.

For she knew Hugh Shardlow, Duke of Martock, could kiss away all her concerns. He could whisper sweet nothings into her ears until she forgot all the lies, all the distrust. She knew he could win her back in a heartbeat.

Her heart skipped a beat. But that wouldn't be real love, would it?

"And if we had found your brother—"

Beth's resolve sharpened. "If? You mean when?"

Hugh stared, a small furrow appearing between his eyes. "What do you mean—you're about to get on a ship back to England."

"Only to retrieve reinforcements," Beth said decidedly.

Well, she had not intended to come back, but she had to now. How had she allowed herself to give up on Matthew? Oh, it was this intoxication with Hugh that had done it. She had lost sight of why she had come here—why she needed to return.

"Reinforcements?"

Beth drew herself up. "It may come as a surprise to you, Your Grace, but you are not the only duke I know."

"Not the only—"

"Yes, my sister married a duke last month," she said, trying to channel her outrage into her voice. "I am certain the Duke of Sedley will provide me with—"

"The Duke of Sedley?" Hugh had taken another step forward.

Beth's breath caught in her throat as she saw they were now only inches apart. What was the man playing at?

"It appears I am not the only one keeping secrets."

Beth blanched. "My brother-in-law is a duke, but you never asked about—"

"Please stay."

She blinked. "Stay?"

"Here, in France, with me," said Hugh in a rush. "I'll marry you—please marry me, Beth, and we can—"

And that was what did it. That made her decision for her.

Beth stared at the man as he continued to bluster on about the life they could lead together, away from society, away from all the watching eyes.

Did the man honestly think she could so easily break ties with her family? Abandon them, leave them behind? Ignore the fact that she had come all this way for her brother? That her sister was probably beside herself with worry?

"—it'll be like this argument never happened, you'll know all about me—"

"Last call for England!"

"Goodbye, Your Grace," Beth said quietly.

She stepped around him and toward the captain who had just yelled across the docks, but not swiftly enough. As she approached the gangplank, Hugh grabbed her arm.

"Beth—"

"Let go of me," Beth said darkly.

Hugh met her gaze and immediately withdrew his hand. "I just—"

"How much is passage?" she asked the captain.

She paid his price, handing over the coins carefully, ensuring she was not overpaying. Oh, the man was overcharging her, but that was merely because she was an Englishwoman.

Beth placed a foot on the gangplank.

"Beth, we can talk on the crossing, but—"

"I am so sorry," she said with ice in her voice, turning to look at the stricken duke. "You cannot come up here; you do not appear to have paid for your passage."

Hugh stared. Then he laughed. "I—I beg your pardon?"

"Has this man paid for his passage, Captain?" Beth asked the Frenchman still standing on the dock.

The captain shook his head.

"Well, there you have it," said Beth briskly. "As I said. Good-bye, Your Grace."

"But you—you're not going to leave me here, are you?" Hugh shouted, his voice almost caught by the wind.

If Beth had taken more than the three steps she already had, she may not have heard him. As it was, the words sank into her chest and caused a chill.

*"But you —you're not going to leave me here, are you?"*

"I—"

"Beth, please, I love you," pleaded Hugh.

Beth's heart skipped a beat. It was precisely what she had wanted to hear the moment they had first kissed. She may not have known it then, but she could see it now. She craved him, needed Hugh in a way she had never needed anyone else.

But she also needed honesty. She needed truth. She had a price, everyone did, but it wasn't this.

"I have no reason to take you with me," Beth said, hating every word but knowing them to be true. "I hope you enjoy your time in France, Your Grace. It may be a long one."

And without a second glance at the gentleman who had taken her innocence and to whom she had given her heart, Beth boarded the ship that would take her back to the people who truly loved her.

# CHAPTER SEVENTEEN

*October 13, 1810*

"ANOTHER," MUTTERED HUGH, slamming the empty glass onto the table.

He looked blearily around him. He could have sworn there was someone serving drinks—or at the very least, pouring this disgusting ale from a pitcher into his glass.

It was unpalatable stuff, yet he had managed, now that he came to think of it, to drink a great deal.

Perhaps that was why the table was tilted. Or was that him?

Hugh shook his head, attempting to see whether it was the world, the table, or his own head which had this very strange angle. The trouble was, when he shook his head, the whole world spun for a moment. The effect was dizzying and most unconducive to rational thought.

"Oh, hell," Hugh mumbled, lifting his empty hand to his head. "I need another drink."

"And how, precisely, are you going to pay for that?" sneered the barman in French, shouting from across the room.

Hugh scowled. He'd never had to worry about this sort of nonsense before. When in London, the Dulverton Club had a tab open for him all the time. He paid it off, too, he thought muzzily.

Regularly. Or at least, his steward probably did. Or was it his butler?

The point was he'd never been denied a drink due to lack of funds before.

But that was before. This was now. Hugh could not understand how he had managed to lose so swiftly everything he had somehow gained.

*"I have no reason to take you with me. I hope you enjoy your time in France, Your Grace. It may be a long one."*

"I'll play for it," Hugh said.

He spoke partly to reply to the barman, who was shaking his head. Partly to push aside painful memories. Memories not willing to let him go.

All he had wanted was to be with her. Beth. She was so beautiful, so elegant, so raucous. There was a boldness in her which had appealed to him, to his very heart and soul.

And he had lost her.

"You won't be winning anything," sniggered a Frenchman at the next table. "You've been in here for days and I've never seen you win."

Hugh tried to smile. That was because he never played cards where he drank. Never a good idea in England, and certainly not something to do in France. He wasn't a cheat. Not precisely. Now that he had nothing else to lose, there was no point in trying.

Jingling the coins in his pocket, he fixed the man with a stare. "I've already done my winning. Another drink!"

It appeared the mere sound of coins was enough to convince the serving maid. She stepped over with a scowl. The ale poured from her pitcher and then she was gone.

"Afraid you've got wandering hands," leered the Frenchman. "English scum."

Hugh allowed it to pass. Perhaps a few days ago, his pride in his country would have forced him to argue with the man. Perhaps his own personal pride would have prompted him to defend himself, if not the rest of his countrymen.

But not now. How could he defend himself when he had done the indefensible? How could he fight for his honor when he had none left?

"Be quiet," was all he could manage.

Hugh hung his head as the drinkers in the inn guffawed.

Well, they had every right to. Here he was, a duke, a nobleman of England. Drinking. Alone. In a French inn. With no way home.

Hugh's heart contracted.

Well, she was quite within her right to leave him here. In a way, Hugh was proud of her. It took real strength of character to do that, stand against a man once you knew him to be a duke.

It was perhaps why he liked her so much. Beth Mead had been unimpressed with him before she had known of his title, and been just as unimpressed when she had discovered it. He had tried to fool himself into thinking that she would be enthralled.

*Enthralled!*

He snorted, shaking his head as he raised his glass to drink once again. No, Beth was a stronger character than that. With stronger morals. With greater standards than he'd ever had.

Hugh's heart sank as he swiftly reached the end of his drink.

Well, what was he supposed to do now?

He could try to win enough coin to return to England, though that would take time. For a moment, Hugh considered it. Spending the next, oh, several weeks trying to trick men out of their money through cards. It had an appealing quality, but at any moment, he would he found out. Caught, in France. As an Englishman, that wouldn't bode particularly well.

And that left the option of...nothing. There was no other option. Other than staying here, wallowing in his own misery.

Hugh's jaw tightened. That hardly seemed to matter anymore. Getting to England was important, but only because Beth was there. He'd lost his chance to return home, but that didn't matter. He had lost something of far more importance, something far more precious.

Hugh forced back tears threatening to fall. He was not going to allow himself to weep openly anywhere, let alone in a French inn.

But it was difficult. The agony of losing her, of risking her affections when he could have told her the truth at any moment…

He would never cease regretting it. Never stop wondering just how close he had been to true happiness. Never stop thinking about the woman who had claimed his heart completely.

"—and I told them, you'll never hold him, he's a madman!" someone was muttering at a table two over from his own. "The man's a monster!"

Hugh chuckled darkly. *They* could be talking about him. A monster.

He had certainly acted monstrously to Beth. *She had trusted him*, he thought, pain coursing through his chest. And what had he done? Utterly betrayed that trust.

Hugh had never considered himself to be a man easily bought, but he had sold himself out at the first opportunity.

"They captured him weeks ago, thinking he was a higher ranking officer, but the blaggard is just a foot solider! They're going to feel rather stupid when—"

And the worst of it all, Hugh knew, was that he'd not gotten his wits about him when it had mattered. When Beth had been standing there before him, asking him why he had done this…Hugh had just prevaricated, hadn't he?

Perhaps he deserved to lose her. He certainly didn't deserve to have her. There would be someone else for her, someone in England who didn't pretend to be someone they weren't.

He had tried to pretend he was a good man. How swiftly that charade had fallen apart.

"—and when are they going to make a decision about this Matthew Mead?"

Hugh almost dropped his glass.

Thankfully, it was almost empty and only an inch from his

table. The clatter went unnoticed in an inn full of noise.

Hugh could hardly think, his mind whirring as he tried desperately to pick up the conversation from the other table. Surely it wasn't possible—a trick of his mind, that was it. He had been thinking so much about Beth—

"This Mead is more trouble than he's worth," spat one of the men. "I heard they're going to make the brute disappear before he makes any more of a nuisance of himself."

Hugh's heart went cold.

It sounded as though Beth's brother was being held captive. That did not bode well.

Hugh swallowed, trying to keep his face calm. As though he had not just heard the name of a person he had spent the last few weeks trying to find.

"—church will be locked until then," one of the brutes at the table was saying. "He won't cause any trouble until…"

Hugh rose to his feet. The church. That was all the information he needed.

Striding toward the door, heart pounding and knowing he could be making one of the biggest mistakes of his life, he reached for the door and—

"Oi! You there!"

Hugh froze. How was it possible they had divined his intentions? Had he been too swift? How could they know he planned to free the Englishman?

Turning slowly on his heels, he tried to count the number of men in the place. Eight—no, nine? Did he count the barman?

The barman in question was glaring. "Where do you think you're going?"

Hugh swallowed. He had to lie. Lying had always been so natural to him, so why were the words sticking in his throat? They could hear his heart pounding, couldn't they?

"Just leaving," he said, as nonchalantly as possible.

The barman frowned. "Without paying?"

Relief swept across Hugh's shoulders. He was a fool. He

hadn't paid for his drinks.

Stepping forward, he reached into his pocket and pulled out what he had to assume was sufficient to pay for the ale he had consumed and put it on the counter. The barman nodded.

For a moment, Hugh just stood there. Then he realized he could go. He had to go. Matthew Mead needed him. Something terrible was about to happen to him.

The church was easy to find. The spire stood out in the bright moonlight, and Hugh had a vague memory of passing by the building on the way into the town. It was hard to recall; it had been such a blur. His mind had been consumed with reliving the last conversation he and Beth had shared.

*"I thought if you knew the real reason why I had come to France in the first place, you would not wish to know me. That I would lose all chance to get to know you, for you to get to know me, the real me..."*

There was a light on inside the church as Hugh crept toward it. There did not appear to be anyone else out at this late hour. That still meant, however, there could be guards inside.

Hugh's chest was so tight it was a wonder he was still able to breathe. What did he think he was doing? He was no spy, no soldier. He had absolutely no experience of these sorts of things. No one else alongside him. No plan.

But the thought of walking away after knowing, almost beyond a shadow of a doubt, it was Beth's brother in there...

*"This Mead is more trouble than he's worth. I heard they're going to make the brute disappear before he makes a nuisance of himself."*

Hugh's hands had tightened into fists. He didn't have to be a solider to know what that meant. Matthew Mead was proving too irritating to his captors and would soon be disposed of.

He couldn't wait a single moment.

The church door under the porch was locked, but Hugh did not give up. He strode quickly around the side of the building, looking for another way in. There had to be. His rescue attempt couldn't be over before it had even begun!

After a few minutes struggling in the dark, Hugh exclaimed

under his breath. "Aha!"

There was a small door at the back of the church, so small he had almost missed it. There was a key still within the lock.

Hugh hesitated. He told himself it was so he could catch his breath—he would be utterly useless if he couldn't think. But really, it was cowardice.

This was not the sort of thing a duke did! Dukes...they duked. They dined, hosted, hunted, drank. Hugh was not the best duke, but he at least knew what was expected of him.

This? This was the sort of thing a spy should be doing.

But he couldn't risk leaving, could he? It could be days before he came across some English troops. Even then, he would have to try to persuade them to aid him. In that time...

Hugh's stomach lurched. *In that time, Matthew Mead could be dead.*

The key barely made a sound in the lock as it turned. Pushing open the small door, Hugh took a deep breath and stepped inside.

The church was lit as he had spotted through the stained glass windows, but now that he was inside, he could see only a glow of a single candle. It stood on a pew on the right from where he had entered. And sitting beside it, head hanging in despair, was a man.

A man with the same dark hair as someone very dear to him.

"Matthew Mead?"

The man's head jerked up. "Who's there?"

"We don't have the time—are you bound?" Hugh hissed as he crept over to him.

The man was wearing the uniform of an English soldier, stained and torn. "What's it to you?"

His suspicion was palpable, but Hugh almost laughed. The scowl on the man's face was so familiar, he would have known him even if he had not overheard his name.

"I've been sent by—that doesn't matter, I can explain later," Hugh said hastily.

The last thing he needed was a long conversation about just why he knew Beth. That conversation could come later. Much,

much later.

"We need to get you out of here—I'm an Englishman, I'm here to…well, rescue you," said Hugh lamely.

It did sound rather ridiculous, now that he said it aloud. But it was the truth—and if they didn't move soon—

"I am not bound, merely locked inside the church," said Matthew, rising to his feet, eagerness lighting up his face. "And it appears you have a key."

Hugh nodded. He had taken the key with him, horrible visions of the open door being discovered and locked once more flashing through his mind as he had let himself in.

"Come on," said Hugh in a low voice, conscious that at any moment, the men from the inn could come to end the life of the English soldier who had so irritated them. "This way."

Matthew Mead had to bow his head low to step through the door. Hugh's heart was thundering as he followed. Had he left too late? Was there already a contingent of Frenchmen waiting outside, expecting to go in and murder their captive? Were they walking right back into the arms of the French?

But as he straightened and looked around him, Hugh could see no one in the dark gloom. Only Matthew, who looked exhausted and more than a little starved.

"How can I ever—"

"Run," ordered Hugh. He could hear footsteps—voices. They could be perfectly innocent townspeople, but he wasn't ready to take that chance. "Follow me!"

He was rather surprised to see Matthew obey him—but then, he was a soldier.

Hugh ran behind the church toward some woodland. Every step was painful, lungs complaining swiftly. The cold night air rid him of all the clamminess and confusion of the ale he had drunk. By the time they reached the trees, Hugh had never felt more awake nor alive.

Matthew's footsteps sounded behind him. They were making too much noise, but it was impossible not to. So many autumn leaves had fallen, every step crunched loudly in the otherwise silent night.

"Stop," Hugh ordered.

Matthew immediately halted, pressing himself against a tree.

*That was a good idea,* thought Hugh. He had much to learn.

Both of them were panting heavily. Hugh tried to regulate his breathing, certain whoever it had been walking up that lane would hear them…

But no. The people, whoever they were, had evidently not been sent to do Matthew in. They were safe, for now.

"We have to keep moving," Matthew muttered. "They'll be looking for me the moment they discover I'm no longer in the church."

Hugh nodded, mind whirling.

He had done it. After all the help he had attempted to give Beth, after all her fears she would never find him, after the pain and frustration she felt in leaving…he had done it. He'd found Matthew Mead.

"Which way to the coast?" Matthew asked urgently.

Hugh chuckled darkly under his breath as he jerked his head. "This way. I'll come with you."

They walked in silence for a few minutes. Desperate as he was to speak with Beth's brother, Hugh managed to bite his tongue. They needed to put as much distance between themselves and the village where Matthew had been captive.

After what felt like an age, the man chuckled. "I don't know how to thank you."

Guilt seared across Hugh's heart.

It would be easy, wouldn't it, to accept the man's gratitude? Smile, pretend it was nothing, laugh with the man then see him on his way to England? He would never have to know.

It was just as easy, Hugh thought, to reveal himself and use the coincidence—for that was all it was—to wiggle his way back into Beth's good graces. Show up in London with her brother, claim her affections once again.

But no. He had to be a better man than that. He had to earn her respect, not cheat his way there by using the rescue of her brother. She was worth everything and Hugh would not attempt to impress this way. Tempting though it was. Easy as it would be.

"Please, don't thank me," he said stiffly. "I owe a debt."

Matthew shot him a curious look that Hugh could discern even in the dark. "A debt?"

Hugh nodded. "It…it's complicated."

Complicated was an understatement. But what was he supposed to do? Ask Matthew to intercede with his sister? He'd not descend to such a level.

"We'll have to decide what to do next," muttered Matthew. "In the morning."

"If we keep walking through the night, we should reach the coast by first light," said Hugh, trying to think fast.

Was he able to leave behind his selfish nature?

He placed a hand in his pocket and counted out the coins that remained there. His heart sank. Enough for one passage.

"Fine, fine," said Matthew quietly. "Then we can discuss—"

"There is nothing to discuss," Hugh said shortly, shivering in the cold night air. "You're going back to England."

Matthew stared. "To—to England?"

Hugh nodded, knowing this was the right decision. "Yes. You have a pair of sisters waiting for you."

# CHAPTER EIGHTEEN

*October 26, 1810*

A s BETH STRODE up the steps, legs aching and shoulders sore, she knew the sort of reception she was about to receive.

Relief, of course. Frustration and anger, at least at first. And then tears.

Perhaps not in that order. Beth knew her sister Nancy well, even if she was the youngest, and Nancy was unpredictable when it came to her emotions.

Still, Beth was relieved to find herself outside the residence of the Duke of Sedley. It had taken far longer than she had expected to make her way from Dover across Kent into London. The journey had been difficult, yes, but not more than she could manage.

It was the regrets she left behind in France that made the experience so unbearable.

*"I have no reason to take you with me. I hope you enjoy your time in France, Your Grace. It may be a long one."*

Beth closed her eyes for a moment as she reached the top step and stood before the bellpull. Perhaps she should never have spoken to him in the first place.

*"Ah, there you are. I've been looking for you everywhere."*

Beth opened her eyes. Well, she had done what she had thought was right to find her brother. Maybe if she had found Matthew, it would have all felt worth it.

Sighing heavily and preparing herself for the very worst, Beth rang the doorbell. It took almost a full minute, by her guess, for the door to open.

When the butler began speaking, it was in a dry monotone. "Good after—great heavens!"

Beth tried to smile. "Good afternoon."

"But—but," stammered the butler. "You—we thought you—Your Grace!"

He shouted the last of this over his shoulder.

Beth bit her lip and pushed her way inside. She did not wish to have this reunion on the doorsteps. "It's quite alright, I can find—"

Further words were impossible. She might have attempted them, if not for the blur of a figure who had rushed toward her, pulled her into a very tight embrace, and knocked the wind out of her.

"Nancy!" Beth wheezed, trying to extricate herself from the vise-like grip.

"Elizabeth Mead, how dare you waltz back in here as though nothing has happened!" her sister erupted, tears swiftly flowing down her cheeks. "Weeks and weeks I've been worried sick about you! Disappearing off like that, no warning—"

"She did leave a note," said a calmer, slightly more amused voice. "Hello there, Beth."

Beth tried to give her brother-in-law a greeting, but all the air had been propelled from her lungs. It was difficult enough to catch a breath, let alone say a word.

"Absolutely outrageous! And to think the last time you traveled alone—"

"I'm fine, Nancy," Beth said, pushing her sister away best she could. "Really, I—"

"Anything could have happened to you!" Nancy said, grasping Beth's arms and looking stern. "Out there in the wilds of France, no one to protect you—"

"I had someone—I mean," Beth said hastily.

*Oh, bother.* She had not intended to say that, but she was so tired. She was in sore need of some quiet and the precise knowledge of where she would be sleeping that night.

The hallway of the Duke of Sedley's home had never looked more welcoming. A warm beeswax glow was emanating from the chandelier above and the sconces around the walls. The luscious red carpet was soft under her shoes, a relief after so many roads. The place was warm and there were smiles all around her.

Beth swallowed. Nothing like what she had experienced the last few weeks. This was luxury. This was now home.

So why did it feel so empty?

"And now you are home, which is precisely where you belong, and I hope you never get it in your head to go off gallivanting again," Nancy was saying sternly.

Beth tried to smile. "Until I go back, you mean."

"My dear," said her brother-in-law hastily. "I think it best if we—"

"What on earth do you mean go back—go back, why would you plan to go back?" Nancy said in a rush, not bothering to take a single breath between words. "You can't—"

"Matthew is still out there somewhere," Beth said, her voice breaking.

And in that moment, she hated that the butler was still there, gawping. She hated the two maids who had crept out of different rooms, dusters in hand, to watch the spectacle. She even disliked that her sister's husband was there. Duke or not, this was a private moment.

A moment she had wanted to share with just her sister.

Nancy's expression immediately softened. "Beth, you did all you—"

"No, I didn't," Beth said fiercely, swallowing tears and trying desperately not to think of Hugh. "I just needed better resources, that was all. A few men, Byron can spare them—"

"Byron thinks it would be best if we all repair to the drawing room for tea," her brother-in-law said decidedly, taking her sister by the arm. "Come along—Wilson, a tray—"

"But we can't just leave him there," Beth said, allowing herself to be pulled along by her sister, hardly paying attention to where they were going. "He's our brother, we must—"

"Tea first," Byron said firmly.

Beth blinked. Somehow, she had managed to find herself in the drawing room. It was a remarkably pleasant room, decorated in the latest style, but with all the comfort of the last decade. Cushions galore.

"I feel like…like I've failed him," Beth said, sinking into an armchair by a crackling fire.

She saw Nancy's face fall, the serious expression that befell Byron's, and once again forced back tears.

Part of her knew it was foolish to blame herself. She had done far more than most in her attempts to find Matthew, and indeed, had taken her very life into her own hands at times.

Many sisters would not even dream of such a thing. Some brothers wouldn't.

But that did not change the fact that after all her adventuring, after all the mistakes she had managed to make with Hugh—

*"You lied!"*

The fact remained, Beth told herself sternly, as tea was poured and a saucer was pushed into her hands, she had not found Matthew.

And now she was back in England, in London, in the comfort and ease her brother could surely only dream of. How was that fair?

"I am sorry," Beth muttered to her teacup.

When she looked up, Nancy's face was stern. "Elizabeth Mead, I've told you once, I've told you a hundred times, it is not your responsibility to—"

"We both said we would find him, and we haven't," Beth cut

across her sister. "You can try to console me all you wish, but it won't make a jot of difference, you know it won't."

Byron cleared his throat. "Perhaps if we just drink our—"

"Well it should make a difference," Nancy said smartly, placing her teaspoon on her saucer. "You did a brave thing, Beth, and—"

"If you had been the one to go out there, to France, and spent weeks looking and did not find him," Beth asked quietly, "how would you feel?"

She knew the answer. If there was one thing that was unshakeable about Nancy Mead, it was that she would have cut off her right hand to save one of her siblings. Beth knew that. Nancy knew that.

Nancy opened her mouth, said nothing, then closed it again.

Beth nodded. "I just can't help but wonder…if I had stayed a little longer—"

"Why did you come back?" asked Nancy, taking a sip of her tea. "Wilson, I said the bohea tea, not the hyson!"

Stifling a smile, Beth sipped her own tea. Just a few months ago, they would have been grateful for any tea. Apparently, becoming the Duchess of Sedley did wonders for a woman's standards.

"I do apologize, Your Grace," said the butler with a bow. "I'll inform the kitchen directly."

He left the room, the door snapping.

"There, now we are alone," said Nancy, turning to Beth, all fury about tea forgotten.

Beth almost laughed. She should have known. Nancy would never speak so sharply to anyone about tea, it was not in her nature. No, she wished to clear the room of the last remaining servant. Sometimes she forgot just how clever her sister was.

"You were saying?" Nancy prompted.

Beth looked at her tea. It was easier to look at the beverage and say what she was about to say than meet the eye of either her sister or her brother-in-law.

"I thought, perhaps, if I had stayed a bit longer," she said hesitantly. "Every day I said to myself, tomorrow, tomorrow will be when you find him."

"But you came back safely," Nancy said gently. "And I don't blame you. All those weeks alone in a foreign country—even if you do speak the language well, you must have been lonely."

Beth's mouth went dry. She had not precisely decided what she was going to tell her sister about Hugh. Part of her wished never to speak his name again, to leave behind all those painful memories in France, where they belonged.

But another part of her knew she could not lie about such a momentous part of her life. An awakening to love she had not expected. A hope dashed—

"What on earth is going on in there?" muttered Byron.

Beth blinked, and a noise which had been growing in the background but which she had not really been focused on now demanded her attention.

It was strange. Mutters, and murmurs, then shouts, all emanating from the hall.

"What is Wilson playing at—the man usually keeps such good order," Byron said with a shake of his head. "I will have to go out there and—"

But that was not necessary. Beth gasped, steadying her tea as she jumped at the sudden burst of the door before them.

"Your Graces, Miss Mead!" said Wilson in a breathless voice. "Come and see!"

He disappeared at once.

Beth blinked. What on earth did he mean?

It appeared her sister was just as astonished. "Has your butler ever acted so oddly?"

"No," said Byron firmly. "We had better—"

"Matthew," breathed Beth.

She could hardly believe it. It couldn't be true; it just couldn't be. She had been thinking about Matthew for so long, dreaming about him, worrying about him, wondering where he could be and whether he was safe. That had to be the reason why she saw a man in the doorway who looked like…

The man moved. Afternoon autumnal light danced over his features, dazzling her for just a moment.

Beth blinked. Then she rose, hands shaking.

"It can't be," said Nancy in a low voice.

But Beth had already placed her cup and saucer on a console table and started walking toward him. There was only one way to discover if she was dreaming.

"M-Matthew?" she said, her voice shaking.

Matthew grinned. "I see you two have made yourselves comfortable—which one married the rich man, eh?"

Beth launched herself into the man's arms. Though he looked tired and weary, it was most definitely her brother.

Matthew lifted her up as Beth heard Nancy burst into tears behind her.

"But I don't understand!" said Beth as happiness rushed through her. "How can—I don't understand!"

"Matthew!"

Beth was once again squeezed beyond all endurance as Nancy rushed at the two of them, holding them both tightly.

But she didn't mind. In this moment, breathing wasn't necessary. They were together again, the three Mead siblings, and she never wanted this moment to end.

After struggling for so long, worrying for months, exhausting herself in a foreign land for weeks…he was here. Her brother had been found.

"Now, I want to hear all about it, but first, you need a bath," said Nancy, releasing them both and casting over her expert eye. "You stink."

Beth grinned. "Welcome home, Matthew."

"Yes, I can feel the sisterly warmth already," he said with a raised eyebrow. "And how very dare you get married without my say-so, Nancy! The very idea—"

"I am afraid that is my fault," said Byron, stepping into the hall with a nervous grin.

Beth watched her sister introduce her brother to her husband, and felt a strange twinge in her stomach.

Not because she had anything against Byron. As men went, he was a passable sort, and he absolutely adored Nancy, which said much for him. And having a duke as a brother-in-law was rather fine. She had never expected anything like that.

Besides, it was amusing to watch the shy man attempt to explain to his new brother-in-law precisely why he and Nancy had to get married so swiftly. It was not something Nancy had ever explained to her, but Beth was no fool.

But she could not concentrate on the precise words around her—one question cut through the noise of her mind and escaped her mouth before she could stop it.

"But Matthew, how are you here? How is it possible?"

Her brother did not appear to hear her. "What, really, the Glasshand Gang?"

Beth sighed. It was going to be just like it was before, wasn't it? She was the youngest. It was always Nancy and Matthew organizing everything without her. She had been brought to the fore while her brother was missing, yes, but now she would be immediately sidelined.

She caught the eye of the butler and sidled up to him. "Did you open the door to my brother, Wilson?"

The old man nodded. "Yes, I did, Miss Mead."

Curiosity leapt in her heart. "And did he arrive with anyone else?"

The servant nodded again. "Oh yes, a gentleman, I would say. Tall, blond hair—"

Beth's heart skipped a beat.

No. It wasn't possible. There must be plenty of tall, blond gentlemen in London. It was merely a coincidence, that was all. She would be setting herself up for even greater heartache if she allowed herself to believe—

"Matthew, who did you arrive with?" Beth demanded as she

turned on her heels.

Matthew frowned at the interruption. "I beg your par—"

"Who brought you here? A gentleman?" she asked urgently, stepping toward him.

Could he not see just how important it was that he answered the question?

"Yes, a gentleman," said Matthew airily. "A duke, in fact. The Duke of—"

"Martock," Beth said at the same time as her brother.

Nancy frowned. "How on earth did you—"

"Where is he—Wilson, where did he go?" Beth demanded, striding forward and opening the front door.

There was no one there. Of course there wasn't; Hugh would hardly stay and risk seeing her. He was under no illusion as to how she felt about him the last time they had spoken.

The last time—it could not remain the last time.

"Why, the gentleman departed and walked down the street, to the left," replied the bewildered servant. "But I don't know why—Miss Mead!"

"Beth!"

Beth paid absolutely no heed to the cries of family or servants. How could she? Hugh had been here just moments ago. He had brought back her brother, which did not make any sense but lingered in her mind, turning over and over again as her thoughts raced.

Where was he?

Skirts flying, Beth raced along the street, passing gentlemen who were not him. Then she saw in the distance a man with dejected shoulders and blond hair.

"Hugh!" she cried.

The figure halted, turned, and her stomach lurched. Beth ran on, ignoring all the gasps of passersby and stares of those on the other side of the street, until she stopped, gasping for breath, before the one man she had until moments ago promised she'd never see again.

Hugh Shardlow. The Duke of Martock. He would always be Hugh to her.

"Hugh," Beth panted.

"Dear God, what on earth is it?" Hugh said urgently, lifting her chin with his finger.

His touch seared her and she knew in that moment that it was no use. Try as she might, furious as she may attempt to be, she could not retain her fury at Hugh.

He was a man who had suffered much, and had attempted to overcome it. He had gone to France for ignoble reasons, perhaps, but had he not undone all that by helping her? And though she knew not how, even after she had given up and returned home, he had stayed. He had found Matthew.

He had brought her brother home safely.

"You," Beth said simply.

Her heart was racing, and for a moment, she was unsure as to her reception. She had been so harsh, the last time they had spoken. The pain had been real then, and she could not understand how it had melted away, but it was gone.

All that remained was affection.

"I hope your…your brother is in the health you had hoped," Hugh said formally.

Beth bit her lip. He spoke as though they were strangers. Perhaps it was best that way—if he had no intention to—

"Thank you," Beth breathed, her gaze meeting his. "Thank you, Hugh."

His jaw twitched. "I didn't do it for thanks."

"I know. Because though you may hate to admit it, you are an honorable man," Beth said, just a hint of a smile on her lips.

For a moment, she thought she had gone too far, but then Hugh's lips quirked. "Oh, I don't know about that."

"I do," said Beth simply. "And I—I'm sorry for what I said—"

"No, I am the one who should apologize," Hugh said fiercely. "After all the trust you had placed in me, I owed it to you—"

And Beth did what she had wanted to do the moment she had

realized it was Hugh. Realized how much she cared for him. Realized she could not live without him.

She leaned up and kissed him boldly on the lips.

If she had been worried the kiss was unwanted, she did not have to worry for long. Hugh pulled her tight into his arms; his hands immediately clasped her waist. He deepened the kiss as he tilted her head, moaning at the intensity of their passion.

Pleasure was rippling through Beth, all the pleasure of his kiss and all the promise of more. It was with great difficulty that she broke the kiss and grinned up into Hugh's dazed face.

"I hope you know this means you'll be marrying me," she teased, warmth spreading across her chest.

"I'm not sure about that," said Hugh with a dry laugh. "You're an absolute handful."

"Well, I have a duke for a brother-in-law now," Beth said with a raised eyebrow. "I am sure he can find the money for a substantial dowry."

"Now you're speaking my language," Hugh said, dipping his lips to claim hers once more. "After all, a man should know what he's worth."

# CHAPTER NINETEEN

*October 31, 1810*

THERE COULD NOT be more happiness than this.

Well. Perhaps in a few weeks. When the woman riding alongside Hugh, autumn sunlight shimmering in her raven curls, would become his wife.

"You're looking at me again, aren't you?"

Hugh grinned. "Now whatever gave you that idea?"

"Because whenever you do, I can feel the heat of your gaze on the back of my neck," said Beth with a grin, twisting in her saddle to eye him beadily. "I don't know how you do it."

"It's the power of my affection for you," he teased. "It's a mighty powerful force."

Their laughter made a few other riders along the North Carriage Drive of Hyde Park peer at them curiously, but Hugh didn't care.

Why should he? For the first time in his life, he was out and about in polite society and all the stares were for a wonderful reason. Because he was with the woman who had bought his heart.

"People are staring, you know," she said conversationally as their steeds walked slowly along.

Hugh shrugged. "I suppose they are. Let them."

"It's easy for you, you are accustomed to such notoriety," Beth pointed out, nudging her mare closer to his stallion. "I am not used to…to all this."

By all this, Hugh assumed she meant…well. Everything.

The way they had so swiftly fallen into the habit of riding together every morning. How they spent every afternoon hidden away in his house, kissing furiously. The luxury he had attempted to pour into her lap. The way he had immediately declared that Midnight, his darkest mare, was hers. The looks they received once the news had escaped into society.

The Duke of Martock, engaged to be married? A Martock, from that scandalous family, finding a match with a family of no birth, no wealth, no nothing? A mere upstart!

Hugh had been entertained by the headlines, the gossipy paragraphs in the scandal sheets. Even Beth had managed a smile when she read, quite erroneously, it had all been thanks to her eldest sister's advantageous marriage.

"Thrown into the path of another duke, I think was the phrase," she had said dryly to him only that morning.

Hugh had laughed then, and he chuckled now.

What did he care for society's umbrage? Once upon a time, it would have mattered. It would have hurt, the idea he had once again lived up to the very worst of society's expectations. That he had, once again, followed his father's damned path.

But now he was being written about for a different reason. One he rather liked.

"You honestly do not mind so many people looking?" Hugh asked quietly.

"Far be it from me to restrict their entertainment," quipped Beth.

Joy rushed through him as he laughed. Oh, this woman. He had never thought to meet someone who could make him smile so easily. It felt as though he had not smiled properly for years. Hardly ten minutes could go by without his lips parting in a grin.

Beth saw the joy in the world just as swiftly as he saw the pain. Perhaps together, she could help him see more of the possibilities.

"How are you doing on Midnight?"

Beth made a face. "I am not sure whether she likes me."

"Likes you?" Hugh glanced at the horse. She seemed perfectly calm. "It doesn't appear that you have any difficulties."

"I suppose I am not a natural horsewoman. Midnight evidently has better ideas about how I should be riding," said Beth with a sigh. "It is painful to disappoint her."

Hugh rolled his eyes. "Don't tell me you're going to fall out with your new mare."

His voice lowered, just a touch, as Lady Romeril rode by in her carriage. She met his gaze with a glare, turning to prolong the irritated expression until her carriage turned a corner.

"Why on earth would Lady Romeril look at you like that?" Beth asked, astounded.

"Apparently, she should have been the first to know of our engagement."

"First to—"

"It is just her way," Hugh said heavily. "Lady Romeril prefers to be in the center of society, the first to learn any gossip. Apparently, her snubbing me at every opportunity the last five years wasn't intended to make me feel ostracized. Lady Romeril's words."

It had been all Hugh could do, at the time, not to laugh in Lady Romeril's face, but he had managed it.

After all, the old biddy didn't know what she was talking about. After receiving the Cut from so many in society, he had thought darkly, it was a wonder he had bothered to announce his engagement at all.

He might not have, if Beth had not insisted.

"Don't you worry, I am getting the hang of it."

Hugh blinked. Beth was grinning. "The hang of Lady Romeril?"

"Goodness, no! I meant the hang of Midnight!"

Hugh relaxed. Well, that certainly made a lot more sense. "I suppose it was easier when you were riding in my arms."

Though he jested, he could not help a little sadness tinging his words. Everything had been so much simpler when they were in France.

Not just because Beth had not known his true rank, although that was certainly a factor. No, it was more complicated. In France, they could speak openly, laugh together, even share the delights of lovemaking.

Hugh's loins stirred, and he tried not to think about precisely what he wanted to do to Beth the moment they returned to the stables.

But here in London, they had to behave. They could not be as open as he wished. He couldn't even ride with her in his arms. What would society say?

"And you're disappointed, aren't you?" said Beth, cutting through his thoughts.

Hugh blinked. "I beg your pardon?"

There was an altogether too knowing look on his love's face. "You're disappointed, aren't you? That we cannot ride together as we did in France."

Hugh sighed. "There is no point in attempting to keep anything from you, is there?"

"I would hope not," Beth shot back.

Warmth spread through his chest. It was a glorious day, but rain could have been pouring down in torrents. As long as he was with Beth, nothing else really mattered.

It was laughable now, thinking of his life before he met her. Hugh could hardly believe he had been so lonely, so angry, so bitter.

Now all that had fallen away. He had something in his life far greater than all the pains of the past. If he was careful, he would treat Beth the way she deserved and he would never have any grounds to worry about losing her.

*Except...*

Hugh's stomach turned. Except what he could not control, that was.

"Hugh?"

He looked up. Beth had concern in her eyes.

"It's nothing," he said hastily.

He should have known better.

"If it's distressing you, it is certainly not nothing," Beth said firmly, slowing her steed to match his pace. "Please, tell me."

Hugh swallowed. There was no easy way to put this. Perhaps he should have had this conversation sooner. The truth was, he was afraid. It would give her the chance to rescind on their agreement, and he wasn't sure if his heart could bear it.

"I just…I have shared with you before, even before you knew me, that my family is not respected," Hugh said quietly.

Beth bit her lip. "You did."

"And you must have seen how I am treated by so many here in London," Hugh continued.

The last thing he wanted to do was draw attention to it—but as an autumnal breeze blew, he knew he had to say this.

Beth nodded. "Yes, but—"

"Sometimes I wonder if it would be fair to give you the name Martock," Hugh said in a rush. "You will not be welcome in so many homes, our reputation will make it almost impossible for you to—"

"Hugh—"

"Almack's will be out of the question; you saw how Lady Romeril treated me—"

"Hugh, will you just listen for—"

But Hugh could not stop. The words were pouring out of him, thick and fast, as all his concerns swelled to the surface. What had he been thinking, offering marriage to a young woman as beautiful and vibrant as Beth? Dragging her to his level, making it impossible for her to enter society as she deserved?

"And even if someone does invite you, everyone will be—"

"Hugh Shardlow, are you having cold feet?" Beth demanded.

Hugh blinked. "What? No!"

"Are you absolutely sure?" Beth asked, her gaze fixed on his. "Because forgive me for saying this, but you are acting in this moment as though you do not wish to marry me!"

Drawing his horse to a complete stop, Hugh stared in horror at the woman who meant everything to him.

"That is not it," he said firmly. Dear God, to think he had given her that impression! "It is more…well. The reputation of the house of Martock is so poor, I cannot help but feel guilty. You will, I am afraid to say, have a hard time. This isn't going to be like your sister. The Sedleys are well respected—"

"This has nothing to do with my sister, and everything to do with how I feel about you," Beth said firmly. Then she added, as Hugh swallowed, "Which is that I am completely in love with you, you dolt."

"Beth!"

"Well," she said with a laugh. "Hugh, I gave you myself before I even knew your name. Does that not suggest my affections lie somewhere elsewhere than prestige and power?"

Hugh tried to take a long, deep breath. That was true, he could not argue with that. Beth's affection was evident, had been from the moment they had first kissed. It had not waned in that time, but grown.

And he loved her. Beyond anything. If he had to give up his riches for her, he would.

So why was this so difficult?

"Hugh Shardlow, we are going to make a break with the past," Beth said quietly. She reached out and took his hand in hers. Hugh felt a shock of desire and devotion rush through him. "We're creating something new. You are not your father. That way of doing things, that way of being? That ends with him. We are starting something different."

Something twisted painfully in Hugh's chest, but it was immediately soothed by a balm of peace. Hearing that from Beth? It transformed everything.

He swallowed. "Everyone thinks they know me."

Beth raised an eyebrow. "Well I don't know how. I still feel like I barely know you."

There was no other option but to laugh. "Goodness, should I be concerned?"

"No, I just meant—"

"I know what you meant," said Hugh softly.

Beth's smile made Hugh's heart skip a beat. "We have the rest of our lives to get to know each other. And we'll change, and grow, and we'll keep getting to know each other."

Happiness settled in Hugh's chest. He certainly couldn't argue with her. In the last few weeks, he had discovered so much about himself that he hadn't known. There would be more, he was sure. Every passing day was a day of learning with Beth. He could never see himself getting tired of her.

"Come on, we should turn back," said Beth, glancing up at the sky. "It looks like rain."

Hugh mirrored her. There were definitely darker clouds than when they had left his stables. The two of them settled in a comfortable trot, their horses shaking their manes. They must feel the incoming rain.

He glanced over at Beth and his love swelled. How could he explain how much he cared for her?

"How is your brother doing?"

Beth gave him a wry look. "The man has made himself completely at home with Byron; the poor man doesn't know what's hit him. He only agreed to marry Nancy, now he's got three Mead siblings living with him!"

Hugh grinned. That sounded about right. "I've always heard Sedley was a good man."

"Oh, he makes a fine brother-in-law, and I think he and Matthew get on well," said Beth. "In all honesty, sometimes it feels as though my brother never left. He's still the same idiot."

Hugh stifled a smile. "That's good to hear."

It was, in truth, a relief. He was no expert of course; as he had tried to explain numerous times to Beth, he was no spy. He had never fought for his country, never had to risk his life for everything. The strain those soldiers must go through...

"I was worried," he said quietly, as they approached the Hyde Park gate. "That his time in France would have injured him. That settling back into London would be difficult."

"I think we were fortunate," said Beth as the noise of their horse's hooves clattered about, moving from sand to cobbles. "I was fortunate indeed to have met you. If you had not offered to help me in that inn—"

"You would have found him," Hugh said awkwardly. "Eventually."

"We'll never know that. The point is, you found him," Beth pointed out, the noise of London returning around them as they trotted down the street. "And I will never be able to thank you enough."

"As long as you're not marrying me in gratitude," he quipped.

Though he tried to jest, there was a flicker of truth in his words. Hugh knew he could bear many things. He had, in his time. But he was not sure he could suffer through the indignity of discovering that Beth Mead, the woman he adored, had only agreed to be his wife because she felt somehow in his debt.

Her snort of laughter, however, was enough to put his mind at ease. "Never fear, I'm marrying you for your money."

"I'm being serious!"

"So am I," said Beth, a twinkle in her eye.

Hugh rolled his eyes. "I am merely saying, I didn't do it to— to earn your affections. I did it because it was the right thing to do."

"I know," she said quietly as they turned onto the street of his London residence. "You did it, and that's what matters."

Their eyes met and Hugh was filled with an overwhelming sense of joy. This was what had been missing from his life, though he had not known it. So much of his life had been lacking this contentment. And he hadn't even known it.

He'd known there was something missing. As they trotted through the gates that led to the Martock stables, Hugh looked about him. Wealth, prestige, a title, he had all that from birth. And so he had not known what was absent.

It turned out it wasn't money, or status. It was love.

"I cannot believe I am this fortunate," he confessed, dismounting as a stable hand approached to assist. "No, you all go inside, it's going to rain."

Hugh stepped over to Beth and Midnight as the two stable lads he kept on in London hurried toward the side door as fat drops of rain started falling.

"I knew it was going to rain," said Beth, holding out her hands to him.

Hugh nodded as he helped her down. "You did indeed."

Any further words were impossible. With Beth pressed so against him, Hugh could forget his worry for their future, the rain falling around them. They should get inside.

All he wanted was Beth.

Their kiss began chaste, as they so often did, but swiftly rose in heat and passion. Hugh poured his affection on her lips, his body quivering at the heady sensations provoked by their embrace.

If this could be every day for the rest of his life…well, it would be a wonderful thing.

Only when the heavens really poured did they break apart.

"Let's get the horses inside," Beth said, grabbing Midnight's reins.

Hugh did the same with his stallion, and within a minute, all four of them were inside the stables.

Beth shook her head, water flying. "I can't believe that I thought you a coward when I didn't understand who you were."

Hugh flinched. He could not help it, the word was such a painful one. "Why do you say that?"

"Because of all this," Beth said, lifting a hand to take in the stables around them. "You had all this wealth, but no one to share it with. You had no affection, no reason to enjoy it."

Hugh's heart stirred. She was right. How was it that Beth was able to cut through all his wonderings and immediately identify what was wrong?

"I think I was a coward," he admitted, putting the two horses in their stalls then pulling Beth into his arms. "I only truly became brave when…when I had something to lose."

Beth looked up at him, dark eyes staring in wonder. "What?"

"You," Hugh breathed.

Their kiss was passionate, her fingers tangled together at his nape, and Hugh knew he could hold back no longer. They had been good for so long—weeks. They would be married within days. Surely they could—

"Hugh Shardlow, I know exactly what you are thinking," Beth said, breaking the kiss with dancing eyes. "No!"

"Yes," said Hugh with a grin, moving to kiss her neck.

She did not push him away, her head falling back as her breath quickened. "We need to get out of these wet things and—"

"I couldn't agree more," said Hugh with a moan, his fingers already scrabbling at the ties of her riding habit.

"Hugh!"

"You want me to stop?" he said, lifting his head to meet her gaze.

There was such hunger in Beth's eyes, he was surprised she hadn't already removed his coat and waistcoat. "I didn't say that."

Hugh groaned. Oh, he would never get tired of this woman. "Good. Now, let's move into an empty stall and get you all warmed up…"

# EPILOGUE

*November 7, 1810*

I T WAS HER wedding day, and Beth was glowing.

She knew she was glowing, even without a looking glass, because her cheeks were burning up.

"You don't have anything to worry about," Nancy pacified as she adjusted Beth's veil, which had been pulled in the wind. "It's your wedding day!"

Beth nodded but said nothing.

Yes, it was her wedding day. A day three months ago she would have laughed at. A day a month ago she would have longed for. And now she was here, standing outside the church as bells pealed into the brisk cold air, and all she could think about was what awaited her inside.

Not just Hugh. Hugh was wonderful. If she'd been afforded the chance to see him, talk to him that morning, Beth was certain the nerves rushing through her chest would have dissipated.

Whoever invented this rule that the bride could not see the groom on the morning of their wedding, she thought, had never been married. The fact that she had attempted to enforce it between her sister and Byron was not the point.

Because it wasn't seeing Hugh that was the problem. It was

walking into a church filled to the rafters with people who were expecting her to fail.

"Fail?" Nancy said sternly.

Beth blinked. Had she said that word aloud? "How does my veil look?"

"Don't think you can get away without an explanation, my girl," said her sister sternly. "Why do you think you're going to fail? There is nothing to do, just put one leg before the other—"

"Oh, leave her alone, Nancy," said their brother with a grin. "I think nerves are a good thing. Just before going into battle, I would always think—"

"Today is not the day for your war stories, Matthew!" Nancy snapped as Beth stifled a grin. "Honestly! This day is all about Beth, and all you could think of is—"

"I was just trying to give the girl a little encouragement! Honestly, you…"

Beth stood and watched her two siblings bicker. Strange though it may seem, the sight of them returning to the argument which had consumed most of last night was oddly comforting.

For months, this was what she had wanted. Matthew back with them, safe and sound. So they could return to the loving yet constantly argumentative family they had made.

Their home had seemed so empty after Matthew had gone to be a soldier, even though they had only rented two rooms from Mrs. McCall. Now that he was back, everything felt right with the world. Except…

Beth swallowed. Except the happy home she had enjoyed ever since her brother had been rescued from France was about to end. Not because he was leaving. Because she was.

"Beth?"

She blinked. Both her siblings were peering at her.

She smiled weakly. "Everyone is going to be staring."

"It's your wedding day," reminded Nancy for about the thousandth time. "Of course they will!"

"And they're all happy for you," added Matthew with a smile.

"Why else would they accept the invitation?"

Beth bit her lip. Many reasons, she wanted to say. Because everyone assumed this was a rushed wedding for one simple reason. Because they wanted to come and gawp at a woman who managed to land a duke. Because Hugh was right. His reputation was truly awful, and many were here merely to make snide remarks.

But she couldn't say all that. Partly because she wanted to protect Hugh from the dishonor. She did not want his new sister and brother-in-law thinking ill of him; her instincts to shield him were fierce. And partly because…

Beth hung her head. "I just worry they'll be disappointed in me."

She was swiftly pulled into an embrace by both her siblings.

"Disappointed? In you?" said Nancy. "They wouldn't dare."

"Remember, you are the one Martock decided to marry," Matthew said quietly. "And all the sniffing young misses in there can go hang."

Beth tried to smile, blinking back the tears that surfaced. It all sounded so simple when they spoke like that. Perhaps it was. Perhaps—

"Oh, the organ has stopped!" Nancy said in a rush, gathering her skirts. "I should be in the church—good luck, Beth!"

Beth's stomach dropped. "But—"

"Never fear, I'll not abandon you so swiftly," Matthew said cheerfully, taking her hand and placing it on his arm.

Despite her nerves, Beth was able to roll her eyes. "Only because you're walking me down the aisle."

"I'm your brother, and I wouldn't let you face those wolves alone," he said with a grin.

Beth tried to match his smile, but it was difficult. This was really happening; she was about to step inside this church and become, in a few short moments, Hugh's wife.

*The Duchess of Martock.*

The thought made her stomach lurch again, but there was no

time to think. No time to halt. No time to think whether or not they could merely return home, get out the Martock carriage, and drive all the way to Gretna Green.

Matthew had stepped forward and there was no possibility of halting him. Beth walked alongside him through the door into the church.

And gasped.

The place was transformed. Hugh had promised he would speak to the vicar about getting the place decorated, but this? This was beyond even her wildest dreams.

Festoons of flowers bedecked every square inch of the place. There were candles, flowers, and ribbons everywhere one looked. The colors of lilac and purple were predominant, with creams and whites dotted about, giving the place the feeling of a luxurious palace.

A sudden noise, a rush. Everyone rose as they saw the bride enter.

Beth swallowed. There were so many eyes staring, more than she had ever seen before. She was not a particularly shy woman, but this was beyond even her limits.

"Matthew," she breathed.

"Nothing for it now," he muttered cheerfully. "Come on."

How long it took the pair of them to process down the aisle, Beth was not sure. She was overwhelmed by the scent and sight of the flowers, then the huge number of glaring eyes…

And then she was standing beside Hugh.

"I thought you'd never get here," he murmured, eyes sparkling. "I feel like I've waited for you forever."

And just like that, all her fears, her frustrations, her worries that she would somehow bring even further dishonor to the Martock name…

They were gone.

Hugh was smiling and taking her hand as Matthew handed it to him. And that was all that mattered.

Beth's vision clouded in the corners as the service started. All she could see was Hugh. Hugh smiling. Hugh's cheeks pinking as he solemnly said his vows. Hugh's eyes sparkling as he placed the ring upon her finger.

And they were married.

"—pronounce you man and wife," declared the vicar. "And now we will sing—oh, my!"

Gasps echoed around the church. Beth could just make out the startled gasp of her sister and the guffaw of her brother before her other senses took over.

Hugh had pulled her into his arms and kissed her.

His lips were warm, determined, passionate. His hands on her waist were strong. Beth gave herself up to the scandalous kiss, losing herself in him as rumor after rumor was sparked.

When the kiss finally broke, Beth grinned, her cheeks scarlet. "Well, you were worried about causing a scene."

"At least this is a scene of my own making," quipped Hugh with a laugh as the vicar spluttered. "Time for the Martock name to gain a little notoriety from our love, not our lies."

Beth flushed. It was certainly not what she had expected—but then, she should have known Hugh would continue to surprise her.

She rather expected she would spend the rest of her life being surprised.

The rest of the wedding service passed in a blur. There was a sermon, Beth was sure, though she could not for the life of her recall what it was about. The value of love, perhaps.

She did not need a sermon to be told that. Beth had never understood the true value of love between a man and a woman before Hugh, and sometimes she thought she still did not. The utter peace that came with standing before one who loved you. The way the world felt different, knowing he was by her side.

It was incalculable. Priceless.

By the time they had returned to Hugh's—*to our home*, Beth corrected with a start—the change was starting to sink in.

"Well, the new Duchess of Martock, goodness," said Lady

Romeril archly as she reached them in the receiving line. "And will I see you at Almack's?"

Beth's gaze flickered to Hugh. Well, he had warned her. "Sadly not, Lady Romeril. I am afraid to say—"

"Idiot girl, I am offering to sponsor you for this next Season for a voucher," snorted Lady Romeril. "Honestly, where did you find this one, Martock?"

"Wandering about the French countryside in desperate need of being taken in hand," said Hugh cheerfully.

Beth elbowed him hard in the stomach as her cheeks burned. What on earth did the man think he was doing?

"Ah, Martock, ever the same," said Lady Romeril, apparently nonplussed. "Ah, I see young Miss Cooper. You know she is still unmarried? I will have to do something about that…"

And without another word, she marched off.

Beth rounded on her husband. "What did you think you were—"

"I'm sorry, I just couldn't help it." Hugh grinned, though his cheeks were also pink. "I mean, honestly! You could not tell she was offering you a voucher?"

"How on earth was I supposed to know?" hissed Beth, trying to keep smiling as more guests, all unknown to her, approached. "You know, sometimes I wonder just how much of your scandalous reputation you deserve!"

Hugh squeezed her hand. "All of it, probably."

Beth bit her lip to prevent herself from laughing as an elderly couple bowed and curtseyed before them.

Well, he was going to be a handful, she thought wistfully as they welcomed the last of their guests. But hadn't that been what she had wanted when she had thought about matrimony at all?

A man who not only made her laugh, but made her think. Who challenged her in the best possible way. Who was, at his core, unpredictable. Who loved her.

Beth caught Hugh's gaze. She had managed all three with just the one man.

"Well, thank God that's over," he said as the final guest entered the house proper and they were left alone in the hall.

Beth sat slowly on a chair. "I am sure I was supposed to remember all those names, but with so many faces rushing by me—"

"Oh, I wouldn't worry about it," said Hugh with a sigh. "It remains to be seen how many of them actually follow through on their promises to invite us to dinner. I was surprised not to see Wincham, though."

It was another name Beth did not recognize. "Oh?"

Hugh shrugged. It was only then that she realized just how much the person's presence had mattered to him. "The old Duke of Wincham. I heard he'd had a terrible injury recently, lost a leg. Poor blighter."

"Goodness," said Beth in horror. "Lost a leg? We should visit him—"

"We will, in time," Hugh said briskly. "Wincham's not a man to accept unexpected guests, though. I'll have to write a note. He was always a bit of a recluse, to tell the truth."

"And you are close?"

"Oh, I wouldn't say close," said Hugh, sitting beside her and kissing her hand. "Just another man in society who doesn't care much for it. He's always very good at parties—at least, all the card parties and dinners we've attended, he's been outrageously fun."

"In that case, I may be glad he is not here," said Beth dryly. "The last thing we need is more scandal!"

"I can't imagine there'll be much more of that," Hugh said, slipping an arm about her and drawing her close. "After all, what could there possibly be a scandal about?"

Beth bit her lip, then forced herself to stop. Given what news she had to impart to her new husband, it was a habit she would have to lose...

"Ah," she said helplessly. "About that..."

Hugh leaned back with a laugh. "Don't tell me you have another brother lost in a war torn country! I've only just recovered from the first one!"

"No, it's not that," said Beth slowly, heart skipping a beat.

Was this the right time? *She* could not think of a better. There was such joy already spilling over her heart, and if she did not say the words soon, they too would spill over before she could stop them.

And she so wanted to see the look on his face…

"It's…well. There is another family member of mine who isn't here," she said softly, meeting his gaze.

Hugh groaned. "I knew it! Why didn't you say? We could have postponed the wedding, made sure they could attend—"

"Oh, I don't think that would have been a good idea," said Beth, trying not to smile.

"Why not?" persisted Hugh, looking deep into her eyes. "I know how important family is to you, Beth, and though my family has never been worth anything of note—"

"Well, I think this one will be," Beth said quietly. "I think they'll be rather special indeed, once they arrive in, oh, say…several months."

For a moment, Hugh just looked at her as though waiting for her to continue. When the silence elongated so long Beth was unsure whether she could stand it, she slowly moved her hand, the one that was intertwined with Hugh's, and brought it to rest on her stomach.

The stomach that looked no different than it had a few weeks ago. Yet the signs were already beginning…

Hugh's eyes widened. "No."

"I think so," breathed Beth.

"You—you can't be."

Beth's grinned. "You and I can argue about it while we get the nursery ready—Hugh!"

Her exclamation echoed around the hall as her husband swept her in his arms.

"Oh, Beth! Truly, a baby—you are with child?"

"I think I am, though I will not know for certain until Christmas, I think," said Beth, excitement rushing through her, nerves tingling with exhilaration. "You see now why we—"

"Is that why you wished to marry so swiftly? And here I was, thinking it was my charming and attractive nature," said Hugh with a laugh.

Beth kissed him. It was like coming home and meeting him for the first time all over again. "It was partly that, of course, but—"

"You know, this is perfect," Hugh said, joy coloring his every word. "Beth, I…I said before every duke has his price, but this…this is truly priceless."

He kissed her forehead as he pulled her close, and Beth could have cried with happiness.

"I suppose I shall just have to endeavor to deserve you," she whispered.

"You earned me a long time ago," said Hugh fiercely, his love pouring out of him. "Now I'll just have to ensure I've earned this happiness."

# About Emily E K Murdoch

If you love falling in love, then you've come to the right place.

I am a historian and writer and have a varied career to date: from examining medieval manuscripts to designing museum exhibitions, to working as a researcher for the BBC to working for the National Trust.

My books range from England 1050 to Texas 1848, and I can't wait for you to fall in love with my heroes and heroines!

Follow me on twitter and instagram @emilyekmurdoch, find me on facebook at facebook.com/theemilyekmurdoch, and read my blog at www.emilyekmurdoch.com.

www.ingramcontent.com/pod-product-compliance
Lightning Source LLC
Chambersburg PA
CBHW061300210726
48293CB00003B/1048